A HERO
DOESN'T ALWAYS FEEL LIKE ONE. . . .

All around me was confusion. I heard shouts and grunts and groans of agony. Looking over my shoulder, I saw that many of our men-at-arms were again in full retreat up the face of the ridge.

I spotted a Templar banner clutched in the hands of a sergeanto, who lay dead on the ground. I grabbed it and raised it high over my head. Waving it back and forth I hollered, "Beauseant! Beauseant!" as loudly as I could.

At first my shouts had no effect. Then I heard a few men nearby begin to join in. Slowly the men who had been running away stopped. With a mighty roar they came charging back into the fight.

I held fast to the banner, brandishing it before me, yelling encouragement to the men until my throat was raw. I felt dizzy and light-headed but knew instinctively that I must keep the banner held high and my sword in my hand if I was to remain alive.

Finally, the enemy lines were broken. The knights and men-at-arms gave a mighty shout. Slowly the dust settled and the horses quieted. All that was left was the carnage around me.

A few moments later Quincy rode up and dismounted, his voice full of excitement.

"Tristan! I saw what you did for the King. All the squires are talking about it! You're a hero! Wasn't our victory glorious?" he asked excitedly.

It didn't feel glorious. It didn't feel glorious at all.

OTHER BOOKS YOU MAY ENJOY

THE
YOUNGEST
TEMPLAR

BOOK ONE
KEEPER OF THE GRAIL

Michael P. Spradlin

PUFFIN BOOKS
An Imprint of Penguin Group (USA) Inc.

PUFFIN BOOKS

Published by the Penguin Group

Penguin Young Readers Group, 345 Hudson Street, New York, New York 10014, U.S.A.

Penguin Group (Canada), 90 Eglinton Avenue East, Suite 700, Toronto, Ontario, Canada M4P 2Y3
(a division of Pearson Penguin Canada Inc.)

Penguin Books Ltd, 80 Strand, London WC2R 0RL, England

Penguin Ireland, 25 St Stephen's Green, Dublin 2, Ireland (a division of Penguin Books Ltd)

Penguin Group (Australia), 250 Camberwell Road, Camberwell, Victoria 3124, Australia
(a division of Pearson Australia Group Pty Ltd)

Penguin Books India Pvt Ltd, 11 Community Centre, Panchsheel Park, New Delhi - 110 017, India

Penguin Group (NZ), 67 Apollo Drive, Rosedale, North Shore 0632, New Zealand
(a division of Pearson New Zealand Ltd.)

Penguin Books (South Africa) (Pty) Ltd, 24 Sturdee Avenue,
Rosebank, Johannesburg 2196, South Africa

Registered Offices: Penguin Books Ltd, 80 Strand, London WC2R 0RL, England

First published in the United States of America by G. P. Putnam's Sons,
a division of Penguin Young Readers Group, 2008
Published by Puffin Books, a division of Penguin Young Readers Group, 2009

5 7 9 10 8 6

Copyright © Michael Spradlin, 2008
Map illustration copyright © 2008 by Mike Reagan
All rights reserved

THE LIBRARY OF CONGRESS HAS CATALOGED THE G. P. PUTNAM'S SONS EDITION AS FOLLOWS:

Spradlin, Michael P.
Keeper of the Grail / by Michael P. Spradlin.
p.   cm.—(The youngest Templar; bk. 1)
Summary: In 1191, fifteen-year-old Tristan, a youth of unknown origins raised in an English abbey,
becomes a Templar Knight's squire during the Third Crusade and soon finds himself
on a mission to bring the Holy Grail to safety.
ISBN: 978-0-399-24763-7 (hc)
[1. Knights and Knighthood—Fiction. 2. Grail—Fiction. 3. Middle Ages—Fiction.
4. Crusades—Third, 1189-1192—Fiction.]
I. Title
PZ7.S7645Kee 2008
[Fic]—dc22   2007036143

Puffin Books ISBN 978-0-14241461-3

Printed in the United States of America

Design by Marikka Tamura. Text set in Centaur MT.

This book is for my son
Michael Patrick Spradlin, Jr.
You have made me a rich man in sons.

Acknowledgments

It takes a village to raise a book, and this one would not have been possible without the help, support and dedicated efforts of numerous individuals.

First I thank Timothy Travaglini, my editor, for his patience and friendship, and for believing in the story from the beginning. I also thank my agent, Steven Chudney, for his guidance and advice. To my writer friends Christopher Moore, T. Jefferson Parker, Mary Casanova and Meg Cabot, thanks for the advice, wisdom and encouragement. And for letting me bounce ideas off all of you when you'd probably rather be writing your own books instead of listening to me yammer on.

I'd also like to thank Naomi Williamson and the staff and volunteers who coordinate the fantastic Children's Literature Festival at the University of Central Missouri each year. They do very important work: bringing authors and children together in a celebration of books and writing. They've given me a marvelous opportunity to reach and encourage hundreds of young readers, and I'm humbled and honored to be a part of the event each year.

My family is the world's greatest support system. My mom has encouraged me my whole life, no matter what I've chosen to do, with a smile and a "That's wonderful, dear!" Thanks, Mom. My sisters Connie and Regina have likely alienated everyone they know by regaling friends, coworkers and strangers on the street with stories of their little brother's writing exploits. To my knowledge no restraining orders have been filed yet. To the two best kids any dad could ask for, I say thanks to Mick and Rachel. And to my wife, Kelly, the greatest wife in the whole history of wives, with all the love and gratitude I can muster for sticking by this big, dumb Irishman for the last twenty-six years. I love you all.

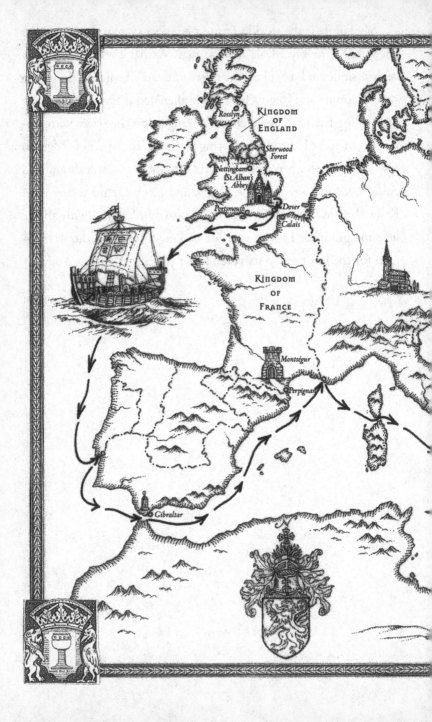

EUROPE & OUTREMER
(THE·HOLY·LAND)
Circa Anno Domini 1191

MEDITERRANEAN SEA

KINGDOM
OF
CYPRUS

Tyre
Acre
Jerusalem

DOMINIONS OF SALADIN

PROLOGUE

This time in which we live will one day be called the Dark Ages. What a fitting name. I have done all I can to stand against the darkness, though I still feel it pressing in around me. I had hoped I would find safety here, but that has turned out to be a foolish dream. I have come so far. Not much farther now. Can I bring an end to this?

I am alone now. Sir Thomas sent me from Acre with a few coins, and I've kept his sword and ring. I have enough, if I am careful, to see me through this duty, but there may come a day when I must sell the sword and ring.

I miss Sir Thomas. He was kind, and there was always food. The work was hard and full of danger, for what is a Crusade but another word for war? He trained me well and was not overly pious like so many of his fellows.

Now I must decide what path to take. I have traveled far and endured much to fulfill a promise to a doomed knight. Should I continue on to face those who would see me dead for what I possess? In the last few months I have learned much about fate. For Sir

Thomas was no ordinary knight. My master and liege, Sir Thomas Leux, served his God as a member of the Knights Templar. And in the simple leather satchel that never leaves my shoulder, I, a mere orphan, an unworthy soul, am now the protector of the Holy Grail, the most sacred relic in all of Christendom.

For centuries legend has said that this simple bowl-shaped chalice caught the blood of Christ as he died upon the cross. And because it once held the blood of the Savior, some believe it to have magical properties. To find it has been the life's goal of countless men.

I heard some of the Templars say that whoever possesses the Grail will be invincible; their armies cannot be defeated in battle. This is why the knights were so fanatical about keeping it hidden, lest it fall into the hands of the Saladin. Truth be known, I do not think much of these stories. If the Grail really makes one's army invincible, then why didn't the Templars carry it into battle and drive the Saladin and his warriors from the field? Perhaps the Saracens have their own sacred relic that cancels out the power of the Grail?

Whatever its legend, even the idea of the Grail is a powerful thing. Though it may or may not be the true cup of Christ, it is a symbol. And in my short life, if I have learned anything, I have learned the power of symbols, from the bright red crosses on the Templars' tunics, to the crucifix that hangs in the chapel of the abbey. Symbols can make human beings behave in less than honorable ways.

No matter the cost, I must now carry this valuable thing to safety. Sir Thomas considered it my duty.

I consider it my curse.

St. Alban's Abbey, England

March 1191

I

hough I am called Tristan, I have no true name of my own. It was Brother Tuck who found me on St. Tristan's Day, nearly fifteen years ago. He is a kind and gentle man, but a deaf-mute, and unable to even write down for me how I came to be here. The abbot, a much sterner sort, tells me that I was found that August night on the steps of the abbey. A few days old at best, hungry and crying, wrapped in a soiled woolen blanket.

I'm told the sound of horses could be heard riding away through the night, but since Brother Tuck was the first to find me, we know not if he saw or even glimpsed the riders. The abbot said that two of the brothers followed the tracks into the woods but soon lost the trail.

He also thinks I must be of noble blood. No peasant could afford to own such horses, and it is unlikely a poor farmer would abandon an infant that might one day grow strong enough to help him work the farm. Nor would any illiterate peasant likely be able to write the note that was neatly tucked into the folds of my blanket. On a simple scrap of rolled parchment, wrapped with red ribbon, it read, "Brothers: We bestow onto you this innocent child. His

3

life threatens many. Remind him that he was loved, but safer away from those who would wish him harm. We will be watching over him until it is time."

So whoever left the note must consider me safe now that I am nearly fifteen. For as near as anyone at the abbey can tell, no one has ever come here and asked about or "watched over" me in any way. Perhaps my parents, whoever they are, were unable to fulfill that promise.

The monks were always kind to me, but they were Cistercians and believed that one was never too young to work. I earned my keep there. However, I bore them no ill will, for the monks worked just as hard as I did. I lived at St. Alban's for all of my life, and my earliest memories were not of the names and faces of the monks, but of chores. We were a poor abbey but grew enough crops and raised enough sheep and goats to get by. Our needs were few. There was wood in the surrounding forest to see us through each winter. The gardens provided us with plentiful vegetables, and the fields gave us wheat, which we turned into bread. If there was ever anything else we needed, the brothers traded for it in Dover or one of the nearby villages.

It was a quiet and calm existence, but the work was endless. The garden was my main contribution to the abbey. Brother Tuck and I tended it from planting in the spring to harvest in the fall. Working the hoe through the soil was quiet work, and gave me much time to think. The garden sat in a sunny spot behind the abbey, and once the rainy spring was over, the weather was usually fine and fair.

Our abbey was on the travelers' road a day's ride northwest of Dover. There were thirty monks in service there. Built many years ago it rose up out of the surrounding forest like a small wooden

4

castle. It was simple in its design, because Cistercians are not frivolous, believing man is here to serve God, not adorn his buildings in finery.

Still, it was a comfortable place, inviting and welcoming to the few travelers who passed our way. The main hall where the brothers gathered to dine and pray was well lighted by the windows that rose high in the peaks. The surrounding grounds were neat and well tended, for the brothers believed that keeping things orderly kept one's mind free to focus on God.

Except for the forest around the abbey grounds, and a trip to Dover three years before, I had seen no more of the world—though that was not all I knew of it. The monks offered shelter to travelers along the road to Dover, and from them I heard things. Exciting things happening in far-off places that made me wish for a chance to leave and see them for myself. Some told tales of wonder and adventure, of magnificent battles and exotic places. Recently, most all of the talk was of the Crusade. King Richard, who some called the Lionheart, carried out his war in the Holy Land, and it wasn't going well. King Richard had been on the throne for almost two years, and had spent most of his time away from England fighting in the Crusades. He was called the Lionheart because he was said to be a ferocious warrior, brave and gallant, and determined to drive the Saladin and his Saracens from the Holy Land.

The Saladin was the leader of the Muslim forces opposing King Richard. He was said to be as courageous and fierce a warrior as the Lionheart, consumed with ridding the Holy Land of Christians. Even those who said that God was on our side conceded that defeating the Saladin would not be easy.

For the monks, the news from the east was of particular interest. To them, the rise of the Saladin was a signal that the end of days was near. Perhaps the Savior would soon come again.

These were my thoughts, on a clear and sunny day, as I worked beside Brother Tuck in the garden. Brother Tuck was a large man, strong and sturdy, with a generous heart. Though he couldn't speak, he made a soft humming noise while pushing his hoe through the soil, moving to some rhythm only he felt. He could not hear the riders approach, or the sound of horses' hooves pounding across the hard ground, or the clang of chain mail and sword as the knights reined up at the abbey gate.

Knights wearing the brilliant white tunics with red crosses emblazoned across their chests. The Warrior Monks. The famous Poor Fellow Soldiers of Christ and of the Temple of Solomon. Known to all as the Knights Templar.

he knights rode through the abbey gate into the shade of the tall trees lining the courtyard. I counted twenty in the group, well mounted, their chain mail gleaming in the morning sunlight. The abbot walked down the front steps to greet the travelers.

"Welcome, soldiers of God," he said.

I stopped working, leaning on my hoe to watch from the garden. I tapped Brother Tuck on the shoulder and pointed to the Templars astride their horses in the courtyard.

A tall, thin knight wearing a gilded cowl dismounted, removing his helmet, and greeted the abbot.

"Thank you, Father," he said. His voice was high pitched and seemed out of character for a warrior. Templars were forbidden to shave their beards, but this one's was sparse, as if he could not grow a full one. His face was pinched as though his helmet were too tight and had forced his features into a permanent scowl. He wore a Marshal of the Order emblem on his tunic, which meant he was in command.

"My name is Sir Hugh Monfort; we are bound for Dover and

the Holy Land." He pointed to another knight, who dismounted and stood holding the reins of his horse. "This is Sir Thomas Leux, my second in command. We have ridden far this day and wish to rest here this evening," he said.

"You are welcome to all that we have, sire," said the abbot. "We are a poor abbey but rich in spirit. I shall have some of the brothers assist you with your horses and you shall dine with us this evening."

Sir Hugh gave the order to his men to stand down. The knights dismounted. Some of them began to stretch, shaking their legs and arms, tired as they were from their journey.

"Tristan!" I heard the abbot call my name.

"Yes, Father?" I asked as I ran over from the garden.

"Make room for our visitors' mounts in the stable, then return with some rope to help them hobble the rest here in the courtyard. They are welcome to our feed and hay," he said.

"Yes, Father," I said.

Sir Thomas, who had overheard our conversation, stepped forward, removing his helmet and holding the reins of his horse in his hand. He was a head taller than I, and a large battle sword hung at his belt. Though his face was covered in dust, I could see a long scar on his cheek that traveled from his right eye down his face until it disappeared in the tangle of his beard. His hair was a reddish-brown color, and an easy smile came to his face.

"After you, lad," he said.

I led him across the courtyard while Sir Hugh remained behind talking with the abbot. The other knights mingled with some of the brothers, waiting for me to return with rope. Our path led around behind the main building to the back where our outbuildings lay.

We kept a small stable there, with a brace of draft horses, two milk cows and some goats. In addition to my garden duties I cared for most of the animals at the abbey.

As we walked toward the stables, the knight introduced himself.

"My name is Sir Thomas Leux," he said.

I stopped and turned to bow, but he waved me off. A knight was nobility, and it was my obligation to bow to him.

"Ah, no need to bow. We don't stand on such formalities in times such as these," he said. "Tristan, is it?"

"Yes, my lord," I said, still partly bowing out of habit.

I noticed that Sir Thomas' tunic was frayed and that his boots were caked with dust and mud. His mail was tarnished, the rust showing through in several places. The shining hilt of the sword that hung at his belt, however, gleamed in the sunlight.

"I beg your pardon, but you seem a bit young to be a brother," he said.

"I have not taken vows, sire," I said. "I am an orphan. The monks have raised me from a babe."

"Ah. Well, you grow strong and straight. It would seem they do right by you," he said.

As we reached the stable, I pulled open the door, taking the reins of his horse and leading him to one of the empty stalls.

"Is the stable your duty?" Sir Thomas asked.

"Yes. Among other things," I answered. "I also work in the garden, I assist the cook in the kitchen with the morning and evening meals and each week I'm required to gather one cord of firewood from the forest so that we have enough for cooking and for the fireplaces in the winter. I also help with the harvest. Then if anything else requires doing, it generally falls to me."

"An impressive list of chores. Are you sure you didn't leave any-thing out?" asked Sir Thomas, with one eyebrow raised.

"No, sire, I'm fairly certain that covers it," I said, embarrassed that I had shared far too much information with a knight who probably had no interest in my day-to-day affairs.

"Well, as for the stable," he said, looking about, "it would seem the brothers have chosen wisely. This may be the neatest, cleanest stable I've ever seen," he added, laughing, as I lifted the saddle from his horse and laid it on the rail of the stall. Removing the saddle blanket, I rubbed the horse gently on its hindquarters. Then I filled the manger with hay and emptied a water bucket into the trough for the horse to drink.

"I'll need to help the others with their mounts," I said, "but when I'm finished with them, I'd be happy to groom the horse for you."

A look of weariness mixed with gratitude came over Sir Thomas' face.

"Don't trouble yourself, lad," he said.

"It's no trouble. I see you ride without squires or sergeantos so you can probably use the help. Besides, the abbot says we have a duty to assist the Crusaders all we can."

"Does he now?" Sir Thomas asked. "Very well then, I accept your kind offer."

"I can show you where the guests sleep in the abbey if you'd like to follow me, sire," I said.

Leaving the stall, I grabbed a coil of rope from a hook on the wall, looping it over my shoulder. The door to the stables had swung shut in the breeze, and as I pushed it open, it caught a gust of wind, slamming backward on its hinges with a bang.

Just outside the door, I watched in horror as Sir Hugh's mount reared up in alarm, whinnying loudly, spooked by the loud sound.

"Haw, haw!" he yelled, taking a length of the reins and striking at the horse as it bucked and tossed near him. This only made the stallion rear again and then jump sideways. When it landed, Sir Hugh lost his grip on the reins and tumbled to the ground. The stallion reared again, landed on four legs and stumbled, crashing into the fence. Its foreleg struck one of the timbers and began bleeding from a small cut.

Sir Hugh lay in a heap on the ground, and while the stallion's head was down, I leapt forward, hugging it hard around the neck with my arms before it could rear again. I calmly whispered to the horse, holding it fast as it tried to jerk away from me. In seconds the horse stopped its rant and stilled, standing with its foreleg gingerly touching the ground. It nickered and whinnied, but had finally calmed.

I let go of the horse's neck and took hold of the reins. Sir Thomas stood in the doorway of the stable with a smile on his face. "Well done, lad," he said.

"Well done? Well done?" shouted Sir Hugh as he scrambled to his feet. "This idiot boy's carelessness lames my horse and nearly kills me—and you tell him well done?"

I winced at his words. Sir Thomas glared at Sir Hugh but said nothing for the moment.

"You stupid boy!" Sir Hugh strode to where I stood. "You imbecile! This stallion cost the Order thirty pieces of gold. Thirty! And his leg is ruined." Sir Hugh puffed out his cheeks, his face a mask of consternation.

"It is only a small cut, sire," I said. "I doubt the horse is lame. Brother Tuck has many—"

Sir Hugh stood there and with exaggerated motion, began putting on his chain-mail gloves.

"How dare you?" he hissed, stepping toward me. I drew back as he grasped the front of my shirt with one hand. I tried to twist away, but didn't dare let go of the stallion's halter, afraid that it might rear again. His chain-mailed fist drew back to strike me and I tried my best to duck, keenly aware that this was going to hurt.

3

xcept it didn't. The blow never came.

"Hold!" a voice said. I straightened up to see Sir Thomas grasping Sir Hugh's arm from behind with one hand. Sir Hugh struggled vainly to free his arm, but could not shake the grip of the stronger knight.

"Release me!" Sir Hugh spat. "I demand that you unhand me this moment! How dare you assault the Marshal of the Regimento?"

"Being Marshal does not give you leave to thrash an innocent boy," Sir Thomas replied calmly.

"That *boy* has ruined my prized stallion."

Sir Thomas released his hold on Sir Hugh but moved around him to a place between us. I did not know what to do. It had all happened so fast. Now I was at the center of a conflict that I suddenly felt had little to do with me.

"I'll be happy to tend to the horse myself, Sir Hugh . . . ," I started to say, but Sir Thomas turned to me with a raised eyebrow. Immediately I wished I'd kept my mouth shut. He turned back to face Sir Hugh.

"I demand that you step aside or I will bring you up on charges!"

Sir Hugh was in a rage as spittle flew from his mouth. It looked at any moment like he might draw his sword and strike down Sir Thomas.

"Do so, and I will bring you up on countercharges of conduct detrimental to the Order. Had the stallion reared again you may have been killed or gravely injured. The boy likely saved your life. The horse doesn't appear to be seriously hurt. I'm sure the monks can apply a salve and bandage to the cut. Now you need to control yourself and take leave." Sir Thomas, I noticed, spoke very calmly. His voice was steady and his tone even.

Sir Hugh's face had gone crimson. I thought it unlikely he was going to change his mind about punching me. His hawklike features were pinched, and the veins on his neck and forehead stood out as he grimaced in anger.

"Sir Hugh, I warn you, lay one hand on this boy, and I will see you brought before the Master of the Order," Sir Thomas said.

"You wouldn't dare!" said Sir Hugh. But his tone had changed. He sounded unsure of himself. His posture changed and he seemed to shrink into himself.

"Then test me," Sir Thomas said quietly.

Sir Hugh glanced over his shoulder. The other knights had now gathered in back of the abbey and stood watching the exchange. Brother Rupert stood holding Brother Tuck's arms behind him as he struggled to rush to my side. I waved at him to stay where he was.

Sir Hugh looked back at Sir Thomas. His face was cold. A look of pure hatred burned in his eyes, but Sir Thomas didn't flinch. He stood there defiantly, awaiting Sir Hugh's next move.

"One day, Sir Thomas. I warn you, one day . . ." He let the words hang ominously in the air. "Make sure that impudent boy takes care

14

of my horse," he said as he stomped off toward the abbey, disappearing up the steps into the main hall with the abbot close behind.

"Sire, I'm sorry to have injured the Marshal's horse," I said.

Sir Thomas turned from where he stood, reaching to stroke the stallion's neck.

"No bother, Tristan. Much ado about nothing. It certainly wasn't your fault. Horses spook. Sir Hugh just has a horrible temper. Let us think no more of it. It might be best if you tended to the stallion though."

"Sire, I do not wish you to get into trouble for my actions, I will explain to the abbot . . ."

Sir Thomas held up his hand to stop me. "You have done nothing wrong. Sir Hugh is Marshal of the Regimento, but it is I who command these knights. Sir Hugh knows he has no respect within his own ranks. He has some powerful friends in high places within our Order and the King's court. But so do I. Nothing will come of this. Think no more of it."

Somewhat reassured by Sir Thomas' words, I led the stallion into the stable, putting him in the stall next to Sir Thomas'. He was still skittish, but after being watered and fed, he calmed a bit. Moments later Brother Tuck rushed into the stable. Taking my head in his hands, he looked me over as if to check for damage. I assured him I was fine, then showed him the small cut on the stallion's leg. He studied the wound, then stepped to a shelf across the stable, bringing me a small earthen jar.

Inside the jar was a muddy ooze that he had created from various plants and roots found in the woods around the abbey. I rubbed a large handful of the mixture over the cut on the stallion's leg, holding it in place for a few minutes while it dried. As an extra measure, Brother Tuck handed me a piece of clean cloth and I wrapped the stallion's leg.

With the horses stabled, Sir Thomas returned to the abbey while I helped the other knights see to their mounts. I finished just as the bell rang for the evening meal.

That night at dinner in the main hall, I took my normal place at the end of the long table. The monks had brought in extra tables and benches to accommodate our guests. Sir Hugh was seated next to the abbot, and for a moment our eyes met and the look of hatred that I'd seen earlier at the stable flashed across his face. I quickly looked away. As I began my meal, I sensed someone at my side and looked up to see Sir Thomas standing there with his plate and cup.

"Might I join you, Tristan?" he said.

"Of course, sire, no need to ask," I said as he sat down across the table from me.

"So, young Tristan, you show yourself to be an able lad. Quick of mind and handy with your voluminous chores," Sir Thomas said.

"Thank you, sire." I blushed somewhat, not used to receiving compliments. The brothers were kind enough for the most part, but not free with praise.

"I'm wondering when you are planning to take your vows," he said.

"Vows, sire? Oh. No. I do not plan to join the order."

"Really? Interesting. So what are your plans then? You must be, what? Nearly fifteen? If you've no interest in the priesthood, what will you do?"

Sir Thomas' boldness unsettled me somewhat. How had he so easily guessed my age? Why was he so interested in my future?

"Well, sire. Of course I have thought about it. I mean, I would

16

like to travel to see places. Other places than here, I mean. I don't know exactly how I will do that yet, but . . . Sire, if I may? Why do you ask?"

"Just curious. Travel, you say. I can understand that. Wanted to see the world myself when I was your age. However, you'll need a way to support yourself, some type of job," he said.

"Yes, sire. I suppose that's true," I said.

"Well, maybe I can help with that. We're riding on to Dover in the morning to rendezvous with the rest of our regimento. As soon as our ships return, we'll resupply and leave for Outremer."

"Outremer, sire?" I asked.

"Yes, we Templars refer to the Holy Land as Outremer. It means 'the land beyond the sea.' So I'm wondering, lad, how would you like to come with me in service as my squire?" He looked at me expectantly.

For a moment, his words did not register. I must have looked a fool as I stared at Sir Thomas in openmouthed wonderment. He had offered me something I could scarcely comprehend: a life outside the abbey.

"I beg pardon . . . sire . . . Excuse me . . . What?" I asked.

Sir Thomas laughed easily. "I believe you heard me, lad. I saw no evidence of deafness in you this afternoon. So what will it be?" His eyes sparkled as he watched me struggle with the enormity of his offer.

Looking down the table, I saw Sir Hugh studying us, his face pinched in concentration as if he were trying to learn what it was Sir Thomas had said to me.

"Sire, I thank you," I finally replied, "but I cannot leave St. Alban's."

"Why not? I have spoken to the abbot and he approves if you agree. I have learned much about you, young man. Since you won't be joining the order, you'll have to leave this place soon anyway. What better way than as a squire to a Templar Knight? You will travel, see the world and serve a noble cause. Not many are given this opportunity." Sir Thomas dutifully ate from his plate of stew and bread, not looking at me while he spoke.

"I'm sorry, sire, but I have duties. There is much work to do in the garden and . . ."

Sir Thomas interrupted. "And the timing is perfect, as I am in need of a squire. Mine has recently left the Order, returning to his family home to assist his ill father. You would do me a great service by accepting."

I was speechless. How could I make such a decision? Give up the only life I'd ever known?

"It won't be easy," he continued. "The work is hard and dangerous. We are on our way to war. Make no mistake about that, lad. But you'll be well trained. I will teach you all I know about the art of battle. It will be a grand adventure."

The brothers often told me that God works in mysterious ways. That his divine presence surrounds us always and that he grants us what we need when we need it most. Did he send Sir Thomas to the abbey at the time that I most needed this opportunity?

Sir Thomas' eyes twinkled and his smile was genuine. In that moment, I felt that I had made a friend for life. Glancing down the table and seeing Sir Hugh frowning back at me, though, I became aware that I had also made an enemy.

4

began my evening chores with cleanup duty in the kitchen. I wished to finish my duties quickly, as I had promised to groom Sir Thomas' horse and did not wish to disappoint him. Brother Rupert was the monk who did most of the kitchen work at St. Alban's. He was from France and an excellent cook. He was also the person I felt closest to after Brother Tuck.

We stood at a wooden table in the kitchen, clearing the leftover food from the evening meal into a slop bucket from which it would be fed to the pigs and goats. Nothing went to waste at the abbey.

"I hear you have news, Tristan," he said. I was not surprised by this. Gossip traveled quickly among the monks.

"I do," I said, proceeding to tell him of Sir Thomas' offer. "What should I do, Brother Rupert?"

"First, I would instruct you to pray. Ask God for guidance. But in the end you can do only what is in your heart."

I was very fond of Brother Rupert, but most of the time his answer to all of life's questions was more prayer. I wasn't sure praying was going to make my decision any easier. I had no idea what my heart was telling me.

Once finished in the kitchen, I headed outside to the stables. Though most of the spring rains were over, it could still grow chilly in the evenings. I wondered what the weather might be like in Outremer.

Sir Thomas' offer had unsettled me. My first reaction had been that I could not leave the abbey. What would the brothers do without me? I was almost fifteen years old. In truth I should have left the abbey last year. It was only the kind hearts of the brothers that had kept me there. If I left the abbey with Sir Thomas, I would be on my own for the first time. I was not afraid of the work, but the uncertainty gave me pause. What if I discovered I didn't like being a squire? Then what? Return to the abbey as a failure?

Unless I took vows, I couldn't stay here forever. And I had no desire to become a monk. I wanted something more. Thoughts of adventure and excitement began to creep into my mind.

Then there was the danger. Sir Thomas had spoken of it. A Templar Knight fought, and there was no question the work would be hazardous. Would I be up to the task? All of these thoughts were jumbled up in my mind.

In the dark stables, the small oil lamp I carried gave off just enough light for me to see. I sat it on a barrel near the stall beside Sir Thomas' horse. Taking a soft rag, I began rubbing down the horse's flanks. He tossed his head from side to side as if he appreciated my efforts. After working over each side, I refilled his hay.

Sir Hugh's stallion was finally calm and content. I tried rubbing him down as well, but he did not enjoy the attention. Perhaps he was not yet fully broken to the saddle.

I checked the bandage on his leg and found it secure. Then a feeling came over me that I was being watched. Suddenly the oil lamp went out and the stable was plunged into complete darkness.

At first I thought a gust of wind had blown out the flame, but the stable was eerily quiet, and I definitely felt the presence of someone else.

"Hello," I said to the darkness. "Who's there?"

No answer.

Without the light of the lamp it was impossible to see anything. I thought I heard the squeak of a leather boot and the slightest clink of metal.

"Sir Thomas? Is that you?"

Still no answer. The skin along my neck and shoulders began to tingle. Something was wrong.

As my eyes adjusted to the dim interior of the stables, I thought I saw the outline of a figure in the stable doorway.

Though I knew the layout of the stable by heart, I stepped cautiously across the dirt floor toward the door. Feeling about in the darkness, I picked up the oil lamp, intending to return to the abbey to relight it from the fireplace in the kitchen. Just as I was about to exit, I felt a sharp blow to the back of my shoulders that drove me to my knees. I cried out in agony, falling facedown into the dirt.

I tried to regain my hands and knees, but as I did, I felt a boot connect with my ribs. I let out a loud yell then, hollering for the brothers. But the stable rested a long way from the abbey, and it was unlikely I would be heard.

The next blow knocked me sideways into the wall, driving the air from my lungs. I groaned, trying to cry out, but couldn't gather my breath.

Still unable to see anything but shadows, and sensing another blow coming, I pulled myself up, using the wall for support. Knowing that my adversary couldn't see well either, my familiarity with the stables was my only advantage. I thought of trying to run out the door, but felt that he stood between me and escape. So instead, I dropped back to my hands and knees and scrambled across the floor into the stall that held Sir Hugh's stallion.

He didn't like me sharing his space and began prancing and making noise. I had hoped this would happen. If I could excite the horses enough, the noise they made would give me enough cover to escape from the stable in the darkness. I rose up next to the horse and made a whinnying sound. It drove him crazy, as he believed another stallion had entered his territory. He began to whinny and snort, kicking at the sides of the stall.

There was movement in the stable, but with the noise I could not tell which direction my attacker was heading. The other horses were excited by the stallion, and they also began to clatter and snort.

I was certain the attacker thought I would climb over the fence separating each stall to make my way toward the front door. I did climb from the stall, but instead of moving to the front door, I moved across each fence toward the rear of the stable, trying to move quietly while the noise from the horses helped hide my movements.

The last stall, which sat deepest inside the stable, had a small loft above it where we stored hay during the winter months. At its rear was a door with a rope and pulley used to lift the shocks of hay into the loft after harvest. I knew that my assailant would hear me as I kicked through it, but I quietly climbed up to it from the stall below.

A few steps across the loft I found the far wall. I grasped the door handle and threw it open. Unhooking the rope, I swung myself out into the air. I heard retreating footsteps in the stable now and thought he would try to race around to the rear of the stable to catch me before I could reach the ground. I gave out another loud shout, hoping that someone would hear. Then I quickly let myself down the rope hand over hand.

Reaching the ground, I was not sure which direction to run. Either way could lead directly to the arms of my enemy. Deciding to chance it, I turned left, yelling again as loudly as I could, and ran toward the corner of the stable. I thought for a moment that I heard footsteps behind me, and perhaps a muttered curse, but I was running as fast as my sore legs and ribs would allow and did not stop to listen.

Turning past the corner of the stable, I could see the abbey ahead. It was almost time for vespers, and candlelight flickered through a few of the windows. I shouted again, but knew that if the hymns had begun, no one was likely to hear me.

My only thought was to reach the abbey before I could be captured. But then another blow caught me across the shoulders, and I fell to the ground stunned, curling up in a ball, hoping that the agony would end soon.

Then I heard a familiar humming, grunting noise. Looking up from the dirt I saw an oil lamp bobbing across the ground in my direction. Recognizing the sound instantly, with one last effort I lurched to my feet and ran toward the light. I heard a curse behind me and the sound of footsteps retreating. In a few seconds I reached the holder of the lamp. And fell unconscious into the arms of Brother Tuck.

he sensation of cold water on my forehead pulled me from my sleep. I was lying on the bed in my small attic room, high above the main floor of the abbey. Five years before, for my tenth birthday, the brothers had generously given me my own little space here in the rafters reached by climbing a small ladder from the main sleeping room the monks shared. It was lighted only by a small circular window at the peak of the roof, with barely enough room for me to stand. But it was my own space and I cherished it.

Brother Tuck was bathing my head with a cold cloth. I was not fully awake, but I heard voices as I drifted in and out of consciousness.

"This is unacceptable. I won't allow him to leave unless I can be sure of his safety," I thought I heard the abbot say in an angry voice.

"I know. But we've discussed it already and you've agreed he will be safer with me," said a voice I didn't quite recognize. Then I fell asleep again, hoping that the next time I woke I wouldn't be so sore.

When I opened my eyes again, Brother Tuck smiled at me and I saw the abbot, speaking to Sir Thomas standing nearby. I tried to remember what I'd heard them talking about, but found I couldn't.

"After what that reprehensible Sir Hugh has done, I am not sure . . ."

Sir Thomas raised his hand to interrupt. "Father, Sir Hugh is not the threat we need concern ourselves with. Leave Sir Hugh to me . . ." Then they noticed I was awake.

"Tristan, how are you feeling?" the abbot asked.

"I'm fine, Father," I answered.

"Can you tell us what happened?" Sir Thomas asked.

I said nothing for a moment. It was odd to see all of these men crowded into my small space. I noticed that neither the abbot nor Sir Thomas could stand upright with the low ceiling, and for some reason—perhaps it was the pain—I found this very funny. I chuckled.

"Tristan?" the abbot asked again.

"I'm not certain. I was working in the stable. I was about to finish my chores when the lamp went out. When I tried to leave the stable, someone attacked me," I said.

"Do you have any idea who it was?"

"No, sire, none. I couldn't see. I was hit from behind at first. Then I just tried to get away," I said.

"You will need to question Sir Hugh," the abbot said to Sir Thomas.

"I can't question a Marshal of the Order when I have no proof or a witness to the attack. Besides, I'm sure Sir Hugh has an alibi. He doesn't get his hands dirty like this," Sir Thomas said with a snort.

"This is abominable," the abbot said. "We are a peaceful order. For Sir Hugh to attack this boy over a minor injury to a horse is unconscionable. Something must be done."

"I agree, but I can't do anything based on conjecture," Sir Thomas said.

After asking again if I was okay, the abbot and Brother Tuck left my room.

"I'm sorry this happened to you, Tristan," Sir Thomas said.

"It's not your fault, sire," I said.

He nodded. "Tristan, in light of what has happened I realize this is not an opportune time to press the issue. However, we ride out at first light. I don't suppose you've considered my offer?" Sir Thomas' face was hopeful.

"Yes, sire, I have considered it, but I have not yet made a decision," I said. Which was the truth. I hadn't had time to think about it.

"Well, thank goodness you are not seriously injured. Perhaps you can sleep on it and let me know in the morning," he said.

"Yes, sire," I said.

He nodded and left the room.

Rising off the bed and groaning with the effort, I walked to the table. Lifting the candle, I looked at my face in the metal reflector attached to the candleholder. I had a small scratch on one cheek and a purplish bruise on my forehead, but otherwise I looked the same as always: a square face with bright blue eyes that peered out through a tangle of light brown hair.

Standing in the flickering glow of the candle, I thought of my life here at St. Alban's. Of how the monks had taught me to read and write. How Brother Rupert had taught me to speak French, his native language. And how the abbot, stern though he was, had a fondness for numbers, teaching me all he knew of mathematics. I remembered how the brothers had worked beside me in the stables and the garden, treating me as nothing less than an equal.

In the corner was a small wooden trunk holding all of my possessions: two extra shirts, an extra set of woolen leggings and the blue woolen blanket I had been wrapped in when the brothers found me. Opening the lid of the box, I took out the small piece of parchment that was nestled in the corner beneath my extra shirts and leggings. It was the note that had been tucked within the folds of my woolen blanket on the night I was left at the abbey.

It had grown worn and wrinkled from the constant folding and unfolding. But I had not read it in some time. That note with only a few mysterious words proclaiming my "innocence" scrawled upon it and the blanket were the only connections to my true identity.

I pulled the blanket from the box, holding it to my face as I often had before. It had grown soft and the color had faded with time. As a young boy, I had tried to memorize the smell, wondering if the blanket still held the scent of my mother or father. There was a time that I believed that if I were to ever find my parents, I would be able to recognize them from that smell. But now, it held no scent at all. It was merely an old blanket, tinted blue and loosely woven, tattered along the edges with a small triangle of one corner torn away. It was the simple and worn wrap of a peasant. But it was mine.

Returning the blanket to the box, I blew out the candle. I did not know if Sir Thomas and his knights could take me to the places where the answers to my questions could be found. Who was I? Did my parents still live? Why did they abandon me? Those were the things I yearned to know, and I knew that I would never find them here. Deep into the night I tossed and turned until I felt my eyes grow heavy and sleep overtook me.

At first light the Templars were ready to leave. Astride their horses, they sat in the courtyard of the abbey waiting for me. The brothers stood on the steps as I came through the door. I had tied my belongings into a roll, fixing it about my neck so that it hung at my side. I had slept fitfully, still unsure of my choice, but in the end decided I must take this opportunity. The brothers would say it was God's will, but I felt it was my own, and thought that unless I at least tried to find the answers I sought, I would never know peace.

I saw Sir Thomas and Sir Hugh standing at the head of the column of riders. They spoke in hushed tones but appeared to be arguing. Sir Hugh finally threw his hands up as he shot me a nasty look, then went to his horse. I guessed that he had just learned I would be accompanying the regimento and was not happy at the news. Sir Thomas just smiled and nodded at me, and he too mounted up.

The abbot's brow was furrowed and his dark eyes gazed intently at me. Brother Rupert beamed and put his hands together in front of him, and I could hear him murmuring a prayer. I found that comforting, assuming as I was that I would need all the prayers I could get on this journey.

I ambled gingerly down the steps, still sore and stiff but suffering no permanent damage from the previous night's attack.

"Tristan," the abbot said. "It would seem that you have made a decision."

"Yes, Father. I have decided to accept Sir Thomas' offer and accompany the knights to the Holy Land."

"Are you sure you feel well enough to travel?" he asked.

"Yes, Father, I feel much better. I was not seriously hurt," I said.

"I see." The abbot was quiet for a moment as he considered me. Then he gave me a rare smile. "We knew this day would come," he finally said. "Admittedly, we did not expect it to happen so soon. But we realized that someday you would leave us. This is a sad day for St. Alban's."

I was moved by the abbot's words. "Thank you, Father," I said.

Brother Rupert stepped forward, holding out a small leather pouch. Taking it I could hear the clink of coins and feel the weight of them in my hand.

"It's only a few crosslets," he said. "We took up a collection amongst the brothers. You might need some essentials when you reach Dover. This isn't much, but it should help."

I was too moved to speak. The brothers had all taken vows of poverty, and any money they earned went directly to the abbey. This "collection" must have come from the treasury. This likely explained the pained look on the abbot's face.

"Brother Rupert," I said, "I appreciate the thoughtfulness, but I cannot accept this . . ." I started to hand it back to him, but his hands closed over mine, keeping the purse clutched in my hand.

"Tristan, you are one of us. We would not send a brother out into the world empty-handed. You have earned this with your sweat and your kind heart. Take it and think no more of it," he said.

Before I could say anything, Sir Hugh broke in. "If you are coming with us, *boy*, make up your mind. We're leaving now, and you have no mount, so you'll have to keep up. Say your good-byes and step lively." His voice was cold, and tinged with something unsettling.

Brother Rupert shot Sir Hugh a rather nasty look for a monk. He squeezed my hands and clapped me on the shoulder.

"Where is Brother Tuck?" I asked. "I can't leave without saying good-bye . . ."

Just then, I heard a commotion to my left and turned to see him coming around the side of the abbey leading Charlemagne, one of our plow horses. Charlemagne wore the ancient saddle that the brothers used on occasion. Brother Tuck beamed at me as he led the horse to a stop before me.

"This is the last of our gifts," said Brother Rupert. "He will get you to Dover—slowly, but you should be able to keep up. There you can leave him at the stable on the grounds of St. Bartholomew. The priests will care for him until our next trip there."

I looked at the abbot, who nodded his approval. Brother Tuck smiled, grasping me in a tremendous bear hug that took me off my feet. He set me down, taking my face in his giant hands, kissing me on each cheek. I would miss him most of all. Though he could not hear or speak, Brother Tuck had an uncanny ability to learn and know what was going on about him. He understood I was leaving, and his gesture of kindness touched me deeply.

I looked at the rest of the brothers. They were my family. "Good-bye. I will miss all of you. I promise I'll return someday. Soon, I hope."

With that, Brother Tuck boosted me onto the back of Charlemagne. As I settled into the saddle, he handed me the reins. Sir Hugh gave the command to move out. The knights were spectacular horsemen, their chargers leaping forward in unison. Sir Thomas had taken a place near the rear of the column, and as he passed by me, he reined his horse slightly, motioning for me to ride alongside him.

I gently nudged Charlemagne with my heels and he began moving, slowly, as he was used to the plow and not the saddle. He was a gentle soul as horses go, but speed was not his gift. I had my work cut out for me to keep up with the warhorses of the regimento.

This docile horse carrying me away to a new life was my last gift from the hearts of the finest men I'd ever known.

DOVER, ENGLAND

6

fter many hours in the saddle the sun moved lower in the western sky. We crested a hill and below us lay the city of Dover. From the hilltop I could smell the ocean. The city, which had been just a small village when I had visited three years ago, had changed much.

On a hill to the north, a large castle was under renovation. I saw men climbing the wooden scaffold encasing the castle keep, crawling up and down ladders like ants. I could see ropes moving, lifting rocks and barrels of sand as the stones were set in place by men at the top of the walls.

Below us the city spread out beneath the white cliffs that rose so beautifully above the ocean. A large marketplace teeming with booths and tents occupied the center of the town. As we rode down the ridge onto the main street leading into the city, I became increasingly aware of the noise.

Vendors in the marketplace called out to everyone. Passing a small inn, I heard the shouts and songs of happy revelers coming from within. The sounds of a blacksmith banging away at a piece of hot steel rang through the air. We were swept away in a wave of bedlam. Even Charlemagne began shaking his head, snorting in disgust at the buzz of activity that surrounded us.

"Have you ever seen a city before?" asked Sir Thomas, noticing the look of awe upon my face.

"Yes, sire, I came here with the brothers a few years ago. But it seemed much smaller then. Not as many people. And quieter."

"No doubt," Sir Thomas said. "War has been good for Dover. Many of the Crusaders gather here to board ships for Outremer. King Richard wants the castle reinforced and strengthened. King Philip of France is an ally for now, but allies can quickly turn into enemies. Any force attacking England by sea would make Dover a likely target, so the castle must be ready and able to slow down any invaders until reinforcements can arrive. When I first came here as a boy, Dover was a sleepy fishing village. Now the fishermen are far outnumbered by the innkeepers and the merchants."

Riding farther into the city, we eventually came upon several large buildings surrounded by a gated fence. Above the entrance flew a banner divided in color, with the bottom half brown and the top half white.

"See the Templar banner, Tristan?" Sir Thomas said. "That flag flies over every Templar commandery. The colors symbolize the heaven above in white, and the earth below in brown. No matter where you travel, you need only look for that banner and you'll be welcomed as a brother."

We entered through the main gate. As we reined up, knights and squires hurried out of the building, calling out greetings. As we dismounted, they began to mingle, talking excitedly with one another.

"Our order has a commandery like this in most major cities

and towns throughout Europe. Any Templar can rest here, train or reprovision," Sir Thomas said.

He was interrupted by the approach of a large man with a full beard that hung nearly to his chest.

"Thomas!" he shouted, striding briskly up to Sir Thomas, clapping him vigorously on the shoulders. He was at least a head taller than Sir Thomas and easily the biggest man I'd ever seen, larger even than Brother Tuck. His arms were as thick as small trees, and his hands were the size of hams.

"You smell like a sweaty horse and you look worse," he bellowed.

Sir Thomas laughed. "Sir Basil, you've grown thinner. Surely you've eaten since I last saw you?" he asked with a smirk.

Sir Basil roared with laughter, patting his large stomach. "Aye, once I had words with the cook. The food was barely edible when I first arrived. We Templars fight on our stomachs, and this kitchen was in the most pitiful shape. Worst of any commandery I've ever seen. Now it has a larder fit for fighting men—I've taken care of that. No more cabbage soup and bread. We have real food now. Meats and cheeses galore! But I've grown weary keeping the cook in line!"

Sir Thomas smiled. "It is good to see you, Brother Basil. Let me introduce to you the newest member of our regimento. This is Tristan of St. Alban's. He has been living there with the monks, and has joined us to serve as my squire."

"Well, well, well," said Sir Basil. "Monks, you say? Welcome, young Tristan, welcome! A squire to Sir Thomas? Did he not fully explain to you? You can't be a squire unless you're serving a real knight! Sir Thomas drinks like a baby camel and fights like a woman.

Why, he's no soldier! In our last battle, I had to lash him to a tree to keep him from running away like a scared kitten. I faced down a dozen Saracens single-handedly while he cowered in the brush. If it's squire-hood you're interested in, perhaps you should ride with me. Then you'll see how a real knight lives!"

I looked back and forth between them, puzzled. It would seem that they were friends, yet Sir Basil had just gravely insulted Sir Thomas.

Sir Thomas saw the look on my face and began laughing.

Then Sir Basil joined in, pounding me on the back. "We're joking, boy, joking! Why, there is no finer knight than Sir Thomas. You listen closely to him and you'll grow up to be the Master of the Order! Welcome, lad! Welcome!"

I'd never encountered someone with such energy. Sir Basil pumped my hand again, then moved off quickly to greet the other knights in our group. His voice drowned out everyone as he moved among them, shouting out good-natured insults.

Sir Thomas grinned as he watched Sir Basil work his way through the crowd. Then he turned to me. "Well, Tristan, there is much to do. First, you should return the brothers' horse to the church stables. Then be back here as quickly as you can. We need to get you outfitted. Our ships depart for Outremer soon, and by then we'll be well into your training. So, off with you now."

The church of St. Bartholomew was not far away, and in fact I could see the steeple from the courtyard where we stood. Sir Thomas took his horse by the reins off to the stables, and I turned Charlemagne back toward the gate.

The sturdy plow horse was tired and moved along without much argument. Dover was alive with activity, and I felt I would never grow used to the noise and commotion. I passed busy shops and inns and shouting vendors in the marketplace. I was assaulted by the smells of cooking meat and smoke from the fires of the blacksmiths' forges that lined the street. Underneath it all there was the unpleasant smell of hundreds of human beings living in close quarters.

In truth I was not watching where I was going, and because of this, I was nearly run over by a column of riders that had burst into an intersection of the street just as I was about to cross through. I had never seen such resplendent men-at-arms, and as I pulled Charlemagne quickly to a stop, one of them shouted harshly at me.

"Watch out, boy. Move that miserable plow horse and make way for the King's Guards!"

I had nearly been trampled by a mounted detail of the King's Guards! And not just any detail, for at the head of the column a rider carried a brilliant scarlet banner on which were embroidered three magnificent golden lions. I had never seen it before but had heard many travelers at the abbey describe it. It was the coat of arms of the King, and as I stared in disbelief, there he was, riding past me on the most magnificent white stallion I had ever seen.

Richard the Lionheart had arrived in Dover.

he news that the Lionheart had arrived spread quickly through the city. The King's Guards had been forced to slow by the crowds of people in the intersection, and the delay had given me a brief moment to study King Richard. His horse was magnificent, as white as a cloud. He wore a gleaming coat of mail and over that a bright red tunic, embroidered with the same three golden lions that flew upon his banner. He wore nothing on his head, certainly no crown, but not even a helmet. His beard was full but neatly trimmed, unlike the manner of the Templars. He carried a large battle sword at his belt, and wore leather riding breeches.

As the people of Dover realized the King was riding through the main thoroughfare, they called out shouts and he waved in greeting. But before a crowd could gather, the riders were gone, and I followed their progress as they headed to the castle gate.

If Dover had been noisy before, the King's arrival had given its citizens even more cause for boisterous shouts and laughter. As I resumed my journey to the church, the news moved visibly from person to person and shop to shop. Several folks called out to me, asking if I knew that the King had arrived, and I answered back that, indeed, I had seen him with my own eyes.

When I arrived at the grounds of St. Bartholomew, one of the priests there was delighted to show me to the nearby stable used by the church. He was familiar with the brothers of the abbey and agreed to care for the horse until they arrived to take him home. I led Charlemagne into his stall and saw that he was fed and watered. I felt reluctant to leave him, knowing that in so doing, I was severing my last connection to St. Alban's.

Charlemagne seemed to sense this as well. While he silently munched his hay, I patted him and he turned, gently nuzzling my neck. It felt as if he knew we would not see each other again and wished to say good-bye.

The priest had stood idly by while I stabled the horse, and he quietly began to fidget and cough. Knowing that I'd taken up enough of his time, I thanked him again and made my way back to the street. I hoped there would be a meal soon upon my return to the Commandery, for I'd grown hungry and thirsty as well. Perhaps I would have a chance to see what wonders Sir Basil had done with the kitchen. Sir Thomas had mentioned that my training as a squire would begin straightaway, but I hoped he'd meant after we'd had a chance to rest somewhat from our travels.

Dusk was falling and the sun danced along the tops of the hills that lay to the west. The streets and buildings were bathed in gold. And the smells of evening meals were everywhere, so much so that my stomach growled.

Approaching the Commandery, I noticed Sir Hugh standing outside the gates with another Templar knight, one I'd not seen before, the two of them speaking in hushed tones to two other men who wore the uniform of the King's Guards. Whether they were members of the same squad that had just ridden through town, or another stationed here at Dover, I could not tell, but Sir Hugh was talking to them anxiously, as if agitated about something.

They stood off to the side of the gate in the falling shadows and leaned close to one another, making sure they could not be overheard.

I did not want Sir Hugh to see me. Before he could glance in my direction, I dodged behind a wagon that stood parked in the street, peering around the side while the conversation went on.

After watching for a moment more and still unable to hear, I saw Sir Hugh reach into his belt and remove a scrap of parchment, which he handed to one of the guards. He also handed them a small pouch that I assumed contained coins. Some agreement reached, the guards nodded, mounted their horses and rode off in the opposite direction. Not toward the castle where the other guards had escorted the King, but west as if they were leaving town.

Sir Hugh watched them until they rode out of sight. He said something to the other Templar, who nodded, and together they disappeared through the gate of the Commandery. I waited a few minutes more, making sure he did not suddenly reappear, then moved from behind the wagon.

Quickly, I entered the compound, wondering what to do with this knowledge. Instinct told me that Sir Hugh was up to something. Then again, he was the Marshal of the Regimento. Surely he could have legitimate business with the King's Guards. Perhaps they were discussing military strategy, or the need for provisions or supplies of some sort.

If I told Sir Thomas what I had seen, would he think me foolish? That I had been spying on his brothers, assuming an interest in something that was none of my business?

Entering the main hall I was greeted by the sounds of the evening meal in progress. The Templars were a much louder crowd than the monks, and the tables were full of noise and conversation. Sir Thomas was seated at the far wall with Sir Basil and some others, so I made my way there.

"Tristan! There you are," Sir Thomas said when he saw my approach. "I was wondering what took you so long."

"He had to give that old plow horse a kiss good-bye!" Sir Basil said, and the table of knights erupted in laughter as I turned red.

"Go easy on the boy, Basil," Sir Thomas said. "Give him a day or two to get his bearings before you unleash that wit of yours."

"Sir Thomas, I wanted to tell you . . ." I started to report what I had seen in the street outside, but before I could get the words out, he interrupted me.

"You'll need to fill a plate and eat quickly—we have important business ahead of us tonight, and not much time," he said. From the seat next to him Sir Thomas picked up a brown garment and handed it to me.

"Once you've finished eating, change into this. It is a servante's tunic. You will wear it from now on as a member of the Order."

"Certainly, sire, and there will be chores, I assume?" I asked.

"No chores tonight, boy; there'll be time for that tomorrow. But eat and change quickly. You'll want to be presentable for an audience with the King."

I looked up from my study of the garment at his face. He had that twinkle in his eye, but I could tell he was serious.

43

"Excuse me, Sir Thomas. But did you just say 'an audience with the King'?"

"Indeed I did, lad. You aren't hard of hearing, are you? I could have the physician examine your ears if you'd like," he said with mock concern.

"No, sire, not necessary—my ears are fine," I said. But I stood there holding my tunic with what I'm sure was a dazed expression on my face.

"Tristan?" Sir Thomas said.

"Yes, sire?"

"Your meal? Change? There's not much time. The King expects us shortly," he said.

Sir Thomas smiled at me. Sir Basil appeared next to me with a plate heaped with food. He placed it at an open seat at the table and beckoned me to sit.

In all the excitement I forgot about Sir Hugh and his mysterious actions in the street. I ate quickly for the food was delicious, but not even my ferocious appetite could keep my mind from racing. I, Tristan of St. Alban's, born an orphan, would this evening meet the King!

fter finishing the meal, another squire named Quincy, who served Sir Basil, showed me to our quarters. Quincy was two years younger than I, but in many ways a miniature version of his knight. Tall and strong for his age, his face was round and his cheeks were a healthy red. He had a ready laugh, cheerfully leading me to my bunk at Sir Basil's request.

"We sleep in an outbuilding on the grounds," he said as we left through a back door of the main hall. It was only a few short yards across the common, past several other small structures.

"This is the armory," he said, pointing to the first building we passed on our way. "Behind the armory are the stables. We sleep here." By then we had reached a small timber building, square and unadorned. Quincy opened the door, leading me inside.

The interior was dark, lighted only by candles and a few oil lamps. In the center of the room sat a long wooden table with benches along either side. Ten straw mattresses were laid around the interior walls. The far end of the building held a fireplace that took up one wall. There were a few windows that would let in light during the daytime, but now it was damp, dingy and not particularly sweet smelling.

"Does it always smell this clean and fresh?" I said.

Quincy laughed, again reminding me of Sir Basil. "Always," he said. "Come. I sleep here in the far corner. The space next to mine is empty. It's yours if you like."

"My thanks," I said.

I dropped my small bag of possessions, shrugging out of my shirt and pulling on the tunic Sir Thomas had given me. It was a dull brown wool garment, hooded, with a rope belt that tied around the waist. A long slit up the front and back would make it easier to wear while riding a horse.

I looked at Quincy, who was dressed in the same simple uniform I now wore. I'll admit that when Sir Thomas had asked me to join him as his squire, I'd envisioned myself wearing a fancy tunic with a red cross and maybe even my own chain mail. I saw now that I'd been wrong to think so.

"Templars wear brilliant white tunics with red crosses and we have to wear these?" I said.

Quincy just shrugged. "It's what all servantes wear."

Huh. Maybe the chain mail would come later.

"We should return to the main hall right away," he said. "We'll be leaving for the castle shortly."

"Are you going to see the King as well?" I asked.

"Aye. I heard the brothers say that King Richard leaves in two days to ready his fleet. We have a week or so of preparations, then we sail to meet him. He wants to greet the regimento tonight. A simple affair, I heard. To praise us for our service and to speak with some of the brothers on what we might find when we arrive in Outremer and such," he said.

"Why are we invited? Isn't it strange for squires to be included in such a gathering?"

"You might think so," Quincy said. "I heard Sir Thomas and Sir Hugh had quite an argument after Sir Thomas invited the entire regimento. But Sir Thomas would not back down, arguing that every member of the regimento puts his life on the line and should share in the thanks of the King. Sir Hugh was not amused, so I'm told."

"What do you know of Sir Hugh?" I asked.

Quincy didn't answer right away. He looked around the room, as if making doubly sure we were alone. He started to speak, then paused for a moment, as though he needed to choose his words carefully.

"I know we only just met, but if Sir Thomas has chosen you as his squire, then I can assume you are a decent fellow. So let me warn you: stay out of Sir Hugh's way. He's vicious and cruel. He made it to Marshal only because of his powerful friends, but he commands by fear. I've heard some of the other squires say that he is suspected of breaking Templar laws—executing defenseless prisoners, physically punishing squires and sergeantos for no reason. But he is careful and calculating and no one can ever prove anything, and his victims are too scared of him to speak out against him."

I thought of the previous night in the stable and wondered if it was indeed Sir Hugh who had attacked me. From what Quincy was telling me now, it sounded likely.

"It's said that Sir Thomas was placed in this regimento by the

Master himself, to keep Sir Hugh in check. Sir Hugh hates Sir Thomas but fears him. At any rate, I'd suggest avoiding Sir Hugh and his toadies. He's dangerous and crazy!"

"His 'toadies'?" I said.

"That's what Sir Basil calls them. 'There goes Sir Hugh with his toadies hopping behind him,' he'll say. He has the support of a small group of knights in this regimento. But Sir Thomas is the one the men will follow. Stay close to him and you'll be fine."

"He does seem very brave," I said.

"Ha, you should hear the stories! Ask Sir Basil sometime about Sir Thomas on the battlefield. My favorite is the one where Sir Thomas and his men were pinned by a force of Saracens in a blind canyon not far from the plains of Jerusalem. According to Templar law, only when we are outnumbered more than three to one may Templars retreat from the battlefield. In this engagement, the Saracens received reinforcements and were nearly five times our numbers. They pushed the Templars back across the field and Sir Thomas gave the order for the knights to regroup a few miles away, but in the dust and confusion the column took a wrong turn, and were pinned in a canyon with no way out."

"What happened?" I asked eagerly.

"The Saracens realized the Templars were trapped and halted their pursuit momentarily, expecting surrender. Instead, Sir Thomas ordered the knights to charge with lances. Sir Basil said they rode full on at the Saracen lines and the Saracens were so caught off guard by this crazy attack they broke ranks and ran. Sir Thomas and the knights chased them clear across the plains of Jerusalem until the Saracens reached their main force. The Templars held the field once again."

"Amazing!" I said. And from what I had seen of Sir Thomas in the last two days, I had no trouble believing it.

We walked across the grounds, finding the regimento gathering at the front gate. It was dark now, and many of the sergeantos carried torches. Outside the Commandery, the city had grown quiet. The marketplace was nearly empty, the shops were closed and the vendors' carts had disappeared from the streets.

Forming a loose column, we walked through the streets of the city. Sir Thomas was near the front with Sir Hugh at the lead. Within a few minutes' time we had arrived at the castle above the town.

The castle gate was open and the courtyard inside was a busy place. Torches and bonfires gave light to the workmen still scurrying about. Several large carts and wagons were being loaded and unloaded with supplies. Men still worked on the parapets high off the ground.

Trailing through the courtyard, we filed into the grand hall of the castle. I had never seen so large a room in my life. The walls were lined with oil lamps. Elegant tapestries were hung every few feet. At the far end of the room sat a large, long banquet table where servants were busy carrying away the remains of what looked to have been a magnificent feast.

The King stood across the room, at the center of a group of men huddled together discussing something in great detail. He was dressed as he had been when I saw him in town, holding a rolled parchment in his hand. A few of the King's Guards stood at attention along the wall behind him.

Filing along the wall opposite the King, we formed loose ranks. Sir Thomas, Sir Hugh and the other knights stood at the forefront of our group with the sergeantos and the squires at the rear against the wall. I found a spot next to Quincy where I could see Sir Thomas and the others. We all waited there for the King to finish his conversation and address us.

His affairs concluded, he dismissed the men he had been speaking with. As they left the room, he strode across the floor toward Sir Hugh and Sir Thomas. The room went quiet, waiting to hear what the King would say.

"Thomas Leux!" the Lionheart exclaimed in heavily accented English. He beamed, pumping the hand of Sir Thomas. "You look in fighting shape. How long has it been?"

Sir Thomas bowed slightly. Next to him Sir Hugh's expression went cold and his eyes hooded. He stared at Sir Thomas with an expression of the purest jealousy.

"Not since you were still the Prince of Normandy, your highness. We gave the French King more than he could handle at Bourneau. And then some."

"I remember. I remember it well," the King said. "Mostly, I have memories of a young knight who rallied the lines, leading the charge that turned the day."

Sir Thomas bowed his head again, looking uncomfortable. "You are far too generous in your praise, your highness," he said.

"He was talking about me!" Sir Basil said loudly.

At that, everyone, the King included, roared with laughter.

"And I can see this scoundrel has not changed a bit," the King said as he shook Sir Basil's hand. "Sir Basil, good to see you, my friend. How are you?"

"Growing smaller by the day, your highness," Sir Basil said.

This brought another laugh, as Sir Basil was nearly a head taller and several stone heavier than the King. When the laughter died down, I noticed that the King had not yet acknowledged Sir Hugh at all. He couldn't have been happy about that.

Then, as easily as it had come, the friendly expression disappeared from the King's face.

"And now, as knights who served my father with such distinction, you have taken vows as brothers of the Temple? Turning your back on many years of service to the crown to pledge allegiance only to the Pope?" The King looked squarely at Sir Thomas. The room instantly went quiet again.

The expression on Sir Thomas' face never altered. But Sir Hugh's did. It changed from jealousy to intense curiosity. He leaned away from Sir Thomas, as if he wished to avoid any association with the knight who now found himself cornered by the monarch.

Sir Thomas stared squarely at the King. Then in a strong voice he spoke. "I would like to think that we serve God first," he said. "That is the vow that all brothers take when they join the Order. We fight for all Christians. Regardless of whom their King may be."

The room was so quiet that if a mouse had sneezed in the kitchen, I was certain I would have heard it.

The cloud left the King's face. He studied Sir Thomas for a moment, and then he smiled.

"Well said, old friend. Forgive my impertinence. I have fought beside you. I know you have the heart of a warrior. These are dangerous times. There is much to do. The King's court, as always, is full of rumor and intrigue, and I must be certain of those who say they will join me in this Holy Crusade."

"Then let our service in this Crusade be the least of your worries, your highness. We are brothers of the Temple, sworn to protect and defend Outremer, and that is what we will do," Sir Thomas said. At his words the other knights gave a rousing cheer, with the exception of Sir Hugh, who clapped unenthusiastically.

"We will drive the Saladin from the Holy Land, sire, you need not worry about that," Sir Basil said.

The tension left the room. The King visibly relaxed, and taking Sir Thomas by the shoulders he said something to him that I could not hear over the buzzing of the voices. But I did watch Sir Hugh. His expression returned to its normal sour tone. He seemed like a spider sitting quietly in his web, watching and waiting before deciding to strike.

"Have you ever seen the King before?" I asked Quincy.

"Not King Richard, but I saw his father, Henry, at a jousting match in Ulster once when I was just a lad. The people there loved him."

"Tristan!"

From across the room, I saw Sir Thomas looking in my direction. He gestured for me to join him.

I was instantly nervous. Sir Thomas kept waving his arm, motioning me toward him. What was he thinking? Why did he need to speak to me now when he stood so near the King of England? Couldn't it wait? Yesterday I was pulling weeds in a vegetable garden. Now I stood not a stone's throw from his majesty the King. It was all too much. Still, I could not disobey. I walked haltingly to where he stood.

"Sire?" I said.

Taking me by the arm we turned to face the King. "Your majesty," he said.

The King stopped mid-conversation with another knight and turned to look at Sir Thomas. He paid me no attention.

"Yes, Sir Thomas?"

"My squire, your highness. I would like to introduce you to my squire, Tristan. He has recently joined me from St. Alban's Abbey. He's a fine young man. Capable and brave. I'm sure he'll be Master of the Order one day," Sir Thomas said.

Sir Hugh cut in. "Sir Thomas, really, I'm sure the King has much more pressing duties than meeting your *squire*." He spat out the word as if he had swallowed a ball of chicken feathers.

The King looked confused, glancing from Sir Hugh to Sir Thomas, but then his gaze fell on me. He studied me as any royal might view one of his subjects. In the same way that one might scrutinize a horse or cow before purchasing it. But then his eyes narrowed.

"Tristan, you say?" he asked.

"Yes, your majesty," I answered. I was dumbstruck, not knowing exactly what I should do or say, but had at least remembered that. I felt Sir Thomas' hand gently push my back, and I bowed.

"You look familiar. Have we met before?" the King asked.

"Met, your highness? Oh no. No, sire, this is my first trip to a city . . . I—"

"I could swear I have seen you somewhere before," he interrupted.

"Well, your majesty, I was in the street this afternoon when you rode through. Perhaps—"

"No, but there's something familiar . . . " He let the words hang in the air.

I stood there speechless, not knowing what to say or do. The King held my gaze and I returned it in kind, but the room felt warmer now, and sweat began to form on my forehead.

"I just met Tristan yesterday myself," Sir Thomas explained. "He's been living at a monastery. We stopped for the night, and I saw enough of his good works to ask him to become my squire."

"Fascinating," said the King, still staring at me.

"Your majesty, please forgive my *second* in command for his ill manners. It is time for us to take our leave. There is much preparation to be made before we depart for Outremer," Sir Hugh said.

Sir Thomas did not reply but only smiled at the King, raising his eyebrows as he did so, as if only he were privy to some joke.

"What? Yes, of course," said the King. His gaze left me, and he turned to look at Sir Thomas again. "It's good to see you again, old friend. I will see you next in the Holy Land. When we take the field from the Saladin?"

"If God wills it, your highness," Sir Thomas said, and he bowed. He pulled gently on my arm, and we left the King with the small circle of knights who surrounded him. I could hear them saying their good-byes.

As we walked across the room, Sir Thomas leaned close, speaking in a low voice.

"An interesting evening, wouldn't you say?" he asked.

I had no answer. Only questions. Why did Sir Thomas see fit to introduce me to the King? And why, when King Richard the Lionheart looked at me, did I see fear in his eyes?

9

he morning after meeting King Richard was my first full day of life inside the Order. After we'd returned from the castle, I felt I had scarcely laid my head upon my mattress before Quincy was shaking me awake at sunrise. After morning mass and prayer, Sir Thomas summoned me to the stables, where I found him examining the front hoof of the bay stallion he had ridden the previous day.

"Good morning, Tristan," he said.

"Good morning, sire," I replied, trying to hide a yawn behind my hand.

"I hope we're not keeping you awake?" he asked.

"No, sire," I said.

"Excellent. Your first duty this morning will be taking my horse to John the blacksmith. His shoes have loosened on the journey. You will find the shop across from the Whistling Pig Tavern, on the west end of the marketplace." He handed me a small pouch and I heard the jingle of coins inside it. "To pay the smith," he said.

Sir Thomas patted his horse on the nose. "His name is Dauntless."

"Very well, sire."

"Step lively, lad," Sir Thomas called out. "There is much to do in the days before we leave for Outremer."

Retracing the steps that had taken me to St. Bartholomew's, I soon reached the marketplace and turned west at the main intersection as Sir Thomas had said. I noticed several King's Guards in full uniform standing about. I wondered if the King was visiting the marketplace but saw no evidence that he was anywhere near.

As the shops and stalls began to peter out, I found myself on a quieter but still busy thoroughfare. Up ahead to my right, I spotted a stone building with a sign cut in the shape of a pig hanging above the door. Sure enough, across the street was a small blacksmith shop. It was a three-sided building, open to the front, and I could see the fire, forge and anvil.

I tied Dauntless' reins to a hitching ring in front of the building. One of the King's Guards loitered down the street, trying to appear casual, with his forearm resting on the hilt of his sword. He appeared to be watching me, but when I turned to look at him, he glanced away, pretending to be interested in everything else around him.

"Hello?" I called out.

"A moment!" a voice answered from behind the building.

So I waited. The shop looked neat and well kept. Looking more closely, I realized it was not three sided at all, but that the front "wall" swung upward on hinges and was propped up by two timbers at either end so it could be let down each evening at closing time.

While I waited, I turned my attention back to the street and noticed the King's Guard walking in my direction. Without a glance at me he entered the tavern.

A few minutes later, the door to the tavern opened and two men staggered out, blinking and rubbing their eyes. They began arguing with each other. They were nearly equal in size, but one appeared to be in charge, and he pushed the other one in anger. The man staggered backward, lost his footing and fell into the dusty street. I tried not to, but he had fallen in such a way that I couldn't help but let out a chuckle.

The one still standing heard me. His head snapped up as he squinted at me. He mumbled something to his partner, who scrambled to his feet. The two of them crossed the street, looking furtively about as they approached me.

"Where did you get that horse, boy?" the one who seemed to be in charge said.

He wasn't big but he wasn't small either, solidly built and perhaps a little taller than me. Long, dark, greasy hair clung to the side of his face, which was home to a scraggly beard. His eyes were red and his breath stank. His companion looked to be in even worse shape. He had lighter skin but hair so full of dirt and grime it was hard to discern its original color.

"Why do you ask?" I replied.

"Where did you get that horse?" he demanded.

"This horse belongs to my liege, Sir Thomas Leux of the Knights Templar. I don't know what concern it is—"

Dark Hair regarded me through one eye, his other closed and his face scrunched up as if his vision wasn't working correctly.

"It's my concern," he interrupted, "because I think you're lying. I think I should report you to the constables."

"As you wish," I said.

The brothers had taught me much about the evil of drink. However, I had never met or seen anyone drunk before, so I had no idea of the effect that liquor had on men.

I turned, intending to take refuge on the other side of Dauntless, hoping the men would lose interest and move on, or that the blacksmith might show up. But as I did, arms suddenly grabbed me from behind and a foul-smelling mouth hissed in my ear.

"I'll do better than that. I'll just take the horse to the constable myself. I'm sure a Templar would pay a handsome reward for the return of his stolen mount."

"I didn't steal . . . ," I started to say, but the arms squeezed harder and the words died in my throat as the air rushed out of my lungs.

I tried pulling away, but the grip grew stronger as I wiggled and threw myself back and forth, trying to break free. I was lifted off the ground, my legs kicking uselessly in the air.

From the corner of my eye I saw the light-haired man reach out to untie Dauntless' reins. I kicked out with my foot and felt his fingers crunch between my boot and the post.

The man howled in pain and rage, and the next thing I knew I was on the ground and two sets of legs were kicking at me. I tried to regain my feet, scrambling toward Dauntless. But he was beginning to spook, moving his legs back and forth, whinnying and pawing nervously at the ground. Not wishing to be accidentally kicked in the head by a stallion, all I could think to do was to roll up into a ball, hoping they would tire from their exertion before I was seriously injured.

With my face nearly buried in the dirt of the street, I saw a third pair of legs approaching the two men from behind. Had they found another man to come and help them in their thievery?

Instead, I heard both men yelp, and in an instant the kicks stopped. A booming voice exclaimed, "Enough! What kind of men are you? I told you once before that if you molested one of my customers again, you'd lose a finger on my anvil!"

Neither man replied. I looked up from my spot in the dirt to see them both hanging from the air. Behind them stood a giant, holding the men by their shirt collars, which were twisted up around their necks so tightly their faces were turning blue.

Without further word he took a few steps up the street in the direction of the marketplace and tossed them to the ground. As they scrambled to their feet, he gave each one a swift, hard kick in their hind parts.

"If I see either of you on this street again, you'll wish you had never been born!"

Running, they disappeared from sight as the giant bellowed a few more warnings after them. He then turned and walked back to where I lay wheezing in the street.

As he stood above me, his head and shoulders blotted out the morning sun. A huge hand, attached to the largest arm I'd ever seen, reached down and pulled me to my feet. "Since this horse tied here is Dauntless, you must be Sir Thomas' new squire," he said.

As of the previous day, Sir Basil had been the biggest man I'd ever seen, but he could have slept like a babe in the blacksmith's apron. His hands were the size of geese and his head sat upon his shoulders with no neck that I could see, just a full beard and head of curly, dark hair.

"I am," I said, dusting myself off. "My name is Tristan and I now serve as squire to Sir Thomas. You must be John the blacksmith?"

The giant gave a slight bow. "That I am. My name is John Little. But you should call me Little John. Everyone else does."

That, I could not imagine.

10

ittle John, as he was called, worked quickly as he re-shod Dauntless. For a man so large, his movements were graceful and precise, with little wasted motion. He had an easy way with the horse, talking softly as he moved from side to side, patting him gently on the flanks to keep him from kicking while he reattached the horseshoes. As he worked, he questioned me.

"Where did Sir Thomas find you, Tristan?"

"I've been living with the monks at St. Alban's Abbey," I said.

"I've heard of St. Alban's. Were you taking vows?"

"No, sir. I'm an orphan. I was left with the monks as a babe. Sir Thomas and his men came through two days ago. He asked me to join him as his squire."

"I see," said Little John. He didn't say anything more for a while as he worked. Removing the loose shoe on Dauntless' foreleg, he took it to the forge, pumping the bellows until the coals glowed bright orange. As the shoe heated, it turned first white and then orange in the fire. Moving it to the anvil, he took a hammer from the bench and pounded on the horseshoe several times until it took a shape that pleased him. He plunged the horseshoe into the tub of water, and the steam rose in the air with a hiss. In a few moments the horseshoe was reattached.

"Have you known Sir Thomas for a long time?" I asked.

Little John stood and wiped his hands on his apron. "Aye, for a while. Before Sir Thomas joined the Temple, I was a smith in King Henry's army, attached to Sir Thomas' regiment. After I left the army, I came here to Dover. Whenever Sir Thomas passes through, he makes sure to bring his horses by for shoes. I also provide Sir Thomas with his swords. Come, let me show you."

Little John went through the back door, and in the rear was another workbench set along the back wall of the shop. On it lay a short sword that appeared to be brand new. He held it out to me with the handle forward. "Take it," he said.

I took the sword in my hand, testing its weight. It was about two feet long, and the hilt was wrapped in black leather. I'd never held a sword before, and was surprised at the weight and heft of it.

"First time holding a sword?" he asked.

"Yes, sir," I said.

"Well, I think you'll soon become familiar with them. You'll need to know about swords and weapons where you're going. This is called the hilt," he said, pointing to the leather grip enclosed by my hand. "Those metal pieces sticking out from above the hilt are guards. That metal knob on the end of the hilt is the pommel."

I looked at the pommel and saw that there was a small illustration engraved in it. It showed two knights riding double on a single horse.

"That is a symbol of the Templars," Little John said. "The Knights of the Temple take a vow of poverty, and to share a horse shows that they are willing to do without in service to God."

I nodded in understanding, for I had seen this same illustration in paintings and tapestries that hung in the halls of the Commandery.

"This is a short sword. It is used primarily for self-defense. It is made of fine steel and is very sharp. But it is not meant to stand up to the weight of a battle sword or scimitar: it is for quick thrusts and jabs only, not for fancy swordplay. Go ahead. Give it a try. Swing it back and forth a few times."

I stepped a few feet away from Little John, brandishing the sword through the air in a crossing pattern. I knew nothing of swords, but it seemed a fine weapon. Not too heavy, but it had some heft to it.

"It's beautiful," I said.

Little John reached out and took the sword carefully in his hand.

"Take the grip deeper in your fist, like this," he said. "Make sure that your hand fits snugly under the guards for protection. Here, let me show you."

So Little John gave me my first brief lesson in swordplay, teaching me to use the weapon correctly so that I didn't accidentally injure myself.

After just a few minutes of these exercises, my arm had begun to ache, and I told Little John that I must return with Dauntless to the Commandery. To my surprise he took a scabbard from the workbench, sheathed the sword, then handed it back to me.

"It is yours," he said.

My jaw dropped open. "What? No, sir, I couldn't possibly accept it."

Little John laughed and held out his hand for the bag of coins

Sir Thomas had given me. Taking the pouch, he put it in a pocket of his apron. "There now! You've already paid me! Sir Thomas always hires me to make a new sword for his squires. He ordered this one several months ago, and I've been working on it since his last squire left the Order."

"Sir, I don't know what to say," I sputtered. "Thank you. Thank you very much. It is a fine weapon. I'm grateful for your work."

"It's my pleasure, Tristan—and a word of advice. Keep that sword handy. If you run into a couple of ruffians like you did earlier, don't be afraid to show it. Keep it clean and sharp. Care for it and it will take care of you." He smiled.

"I will, sir. I promise. And thank you again. Now, if you'll forgive me, I must return to the Commandery. Sir Thomas will be waiting. There is much work to be done before we sail."

"Good luck to you, Tristan. Sir Thomas is one of the finest men I've ever known. You'll do well as his squire. Listen to what he has to teach you. Trust him. Good luck to you. I hope to see you again someday."

Little John waved as I started up the street. Every few steps, I touched the hilt of the sword now hanging at my belt. In my mind I saw myself following Sir Thomas and the Templars into battle with my sword held high.

Reaching the crowd of the marketplace I noticed that the guards were still in evidence. In fact there were now six of them, and they were definitely shadowing me. I could not fathom their interest, but something in their manner made me uneasy. I quickened my pace but was slowed by the midday crowd in the market. It is not easy to quickly move a stallion through hordes of people.

As we turned at the end of the road that led to the Commandery, the crowd pressed around us. I took a tighter grip on Dauntless' reins, not wanting him to spook, but compared with the noise and confusion of battle, the marketplace seemed not to affect him at all.

Out of the corner of my eye I noticed two of the guards draw closer, falling into step a few paces behind me.

The crowd was noisy and I made only halting progress. As I came past a row of vendor stalls, a man pushing a cart of vegetables crossed in front of us and I had to pull Dauntless to a halt, waiting for the man to clear out of the way.

Forced to stop, I was about to turn to face the King's Guards directly behind me when over the din of the marketplace I heard a noise that left me frozen in fear: the unmistakable sound of a sword being drawn from its scabbard.

II

rasping the hilt of my sword, I hesitated. I couldn't decide whether to turn and face my attackers or take flight. I felt something horrible was about to happen. When the man with the vegetable cart abruptly moved out of the way, I was startled to see Sir Basil standing in the street in front of me.

"Tristan!" His voice bellowed over the noise. "I was wondering what happened to you!"

A sense of relief washed over me. Taking a quick glance to my rear, I noticed that the King's Guards had disappeared, melting away in the crowd. My breath returned to normal, but the prickly feeling of fear still crawled across my flesh. Why were they following me? Even more worrisome, had they been about to attack me? Were they there to take me into custody? Had I done something in our brief meeting that had offended the King? I couldn't think of an answer.

"Sir Thomas wishes you to return to the Commandery immediately," Sir Basil said.

For a moment, I considered telling him about the guards and what had happened in the marketplace, but I realized that I had no real evidence of anything. Perhaps I had been mistaken? I stood there for a moment, trying to figure it all out. Sir Basil noticed the puzzled expression on my face. "What's wrong, boy?" he asked.

"I . . . I thought I . . . Nothing, sire. Nothing. I will return to the Commandery at once," I said.

"You'll find Sir Thomas waiting for you at the practice field," said Sir Basil, winking at me as he headed off on whatever other business had brought him here. I managed to return to the Commandery, Dauntless in tow, without further incident. I wondered if I should tell Sir Thomas what had transpired in the marketplace. As I reached the practice field, I thought it best to keep it to myself. Indeed I would be hard-pressed to even identify any of the guards who had followed me that day. Maybe I would tell him later, after I had had time to think over the incident more clearly.

The practice field lay behind the Commandery, not far from our quarters. I watched as a knight led his horse through its paces, charging first one way, then the other around a series of posts that had been set in the ground. At last, the knight, who was carrying a steel-tipped lance, rose slightly on the stirrups. He spurred the horse forward, the lance held tight against his side, then thrust it forward through a steel ring that hung from the target. The ring detached from the string that held it and slid down the length of the lance that the knight now pointed skyward. He reined his horse to a stop, then trotted back to the target. Lowering the lance, his squire stepped forward to remove the ring and retie it to the post.

"Well done, Brother Wesley," Sir Thomas called out.

He noticed my approach then. "There you are. I see Little John has delivered my gift."

"Sire, I had no idea. I'm not sure if I can accept such a . . ."

Sir Thomas raised his hand. "No fuss, lad. You are my squire. It is my duty to see that you are properly equipped. The sword pleases you, I take it?"

"Yes, sire, it is a beautiful weapon," I said.

Sir Thomas beamed a smile. "Good. Excellent. Well then, now would seem the perfect time to begin your training. Follow me."

In a corner of the field stood a weapons rack. Sir Thomas pulled a large battle sword from it and handed it to me. It was longer and heavier than my own sword, and I found it difficult to lift, let alone hold.

"You will need to practice and work to gain strength in your arms and upper body," he said. "The battlefield is no place to learn that you can't lift or move something at a crucial moment."

Sir Thomas returned the battle sword to the rack, picking up two wooden practice swords instead, and handed one to me.

"Grip it like this," he said. He held the hilt of the sword out so that I could see how both of his hands curled around it, the forefinger of his left hand slightly overlapping the little finger of the right hand. I took the same grip on the sword and held it in front of me at the ready.

Thus began my first practice with the sword. Sir Thomas was a magnificent swordsman, and after a while, I was covered with welts and bruises from being pummeled by his wooden sword. It flashed and darted at me like a serpent's tongue. If I managed to stop or parry one of his thrusts, he whacked back at me even faster twice or three times.

From that first moment on the field, practice and work became the essential elements of my life. Over the next few weeks, I immersed myself in the world of the Templars, quickly learning what was expected of me. As in my previous life, there was work and plenty of it. After the first few days I learned that whereas the monks concerned themselves with growing their crops and praying to God, the Templars were all about preparing to fight. In fact, Sir Basil said the life of a Templar knight was divided into three stages: getting ready to fight, fighting and getting ready to fight again.

On a typical day, we squires took our weapons practice in the afternoon. It was during such a session that Sir Hugh made another effort to bully me.

We were drilling with the wooden training swords under the watchful eye of Master Sergeanto LeMaire. A squat yet powerfully built man, he was a stern taskmaster on the practice field, but an excellent instructor. On this day he led us through our paces, having us practice swings and jabs, then paired us off to work on sparring. I was teamed with Quincy.

Sir Hugh came strolling by the line of squires as if he were a general inspecting his troops. At first I thought he would ignore me as he stopped to instruct a pair of the squires on their technique. Watching him from the corner of my eye, I had to admit that Sir Hugh was an excellent swordsman, perhaps as good as Sir Thomas. He was graceful and moved well, and I realized he would be a formidable foe in a fight. As he moved closer to us, Quincy and I kept practicing and I tried to ignore his presence, hoping he would move on. Soon, however, he stood next to us, watching as we sparred.

Quincy jabbed at me with the wooden sword. Stepping forward, I swung my weapon to the left with the blade upright, solidly blocking the thrust. He stepped back, preparing to move forward again, but Sir Hugh stopped us.

"That was the most pitiful parry I've ever seen," he said.

His words stung, but I tried not to pay him any mind. "Forgive me, sire. I am new at this," I said.

"No excuse. We are here to fight. If you can't do that, you are of little use. A weak link in the chain like you can get us all killed."

Sir Hugh's eyes bore into me, but I refused to be baited. "Then I will keep practicing until I am the strongest link, sire," I said.

Sir Hugh snorted. "Give me your sword," he said to Quincy. Quincy was uncertain what to do for a moment, but timidly handed the weapon to Sir Hugh.

"Attack me," he commanded.

I was reluctant to move.

"In God's name, boy, I have given you an order! Attack!" he yelled.

I made a halfhearted lunge with my weapon. With blinding speed, he easily parried the thrust, then swung back, striking me solidly across my upper right arm. My arm went numb and I cried out in pain.

"Horrible defense," he said. "If this were a real sword, your arm would be lying in the dust right now. Attack again."

I couldn't feel anything in my right arm below the elbow and couldn't grip the sword correctly. My cry of pain had brought the training of the other squires to a halt, and they and Sergeanto LeMaire turned to watch, stunned, waiting to see what would happen next.

"Sire, my arm . . . ," I said.

"Boy, you listen to me! Attack!" Sir Hugh did not wait for me to move. Taking a giant lunge forward he brought the wooden sword swinging down at full speed. I had only a second to raise my weapon, which I held in my left hand only, moving it into a blocking position.

Sir Hugh's sword whistled down, hitting mine with a loud crack. Because I fought one-handed, I couldn't completely stop it. His blow landed on my right shoulder with a horrible crunching sound.

This time I screamed out loud. I thought my shoulder was surely broken. Dropping the sword from my hand I looked in shock at my right arm, now useless at my side. Tears stung my eyes, but I did everything I could to force them back, not wanting to give Sir Hugh the satisfaction.

"That was terrible. Simply awful! You have no talent at this whatsoever," Sir Hugh said. "These are only practice weapons and you can't even get that right. What are you going to do if you are attacked by someone with a real weapon?"

To my horror, Sir Hugh dropped the wooden practice weapon in the dirt. I watched in disbelief as he drew his battle sword from the sheath at his belt and began swinging it back and forth in the air before me.

"This isn't a game, boy. This is war. We are going to fight. What will you do when it is no longer practice? What will you do when it's real?"

Circling around me he swung the sword back and forth, each time bringing it closer to my face. I glanced quickly about. The squires watched on in silence. Sergeanto LeMaire looked stricken, but being far outranked by Sir Hugh, he couldn't do much.

"Sir Hugh . . . ," he pleaded.

"Quiet, sergeanto!" Sir Hugh snapped.

Raising the sword high, he came at me. I saw it begin its downward arc, and there was nothing I could do but jump quickly to the side. The weapon cut through the air right where I had been standing moments before.

He moved back around me in a half circle, raising the sword again. When his hands started downward, I moved to the side, stumbling over the sword that I'd dropped. This time I fell to the ground on my knees. Sir Hugh's sword swung down again where I had just been crouched before him.

As Sir Hugh completed the swing, he stepped forward to follow through. As he brought the sword up and around again, I saw my only chance.

With my left hand, I grabbed the fallen practice sword. As he stepped past me, I quickly thrust it between his legs at the ankles. It worked perfectly. He tripped on the wooden blade and fell headfirst into the dirt. He let out a shout of surprise and his tunic flew up, covering his head and shoulders.

I quickly scampered to my feet while Sir Hugh shouted and cursed. He jumped to his feet, his face turning crimson and his eyes throwing fire in my direction. I couldn't help but smile, which made his face go from crimson to purple.

The brothers at St. Alban's had always taught me to turn the other cheek. I should have remembered my station. He was the Marshal and should have been treated with the respect of his office. But I couldn't help myself. I had done nothing to this man to deserve this treatment.

"Perhaps I am not the weakest link after all, Sir Hugh," I said. This brought a nervous laugh from the other squires. Even Sergeanto LeMaire snickered behind his hand.

"You think you are funny? You think this is a game? I have had enough of you and your insolent . . ." He stopped talking and raised the sword again. I crouched and prepared to dodge.

As Sir Hugh lifted the weapon above his head, a very large hand

72

came from behind him and quickly tore the sword from his grip. It was Sir Basil. Then Sir Hugh went stumbling forward, tripping over the wooden sword and again flopping into the dirt.

The next thing I knew, Sir Thomas was there, kneeling beside him. Sir Hugh rolled over and started to get to his feet, but Sir Thomas placed a hand on his chest and held him in place. Sir Basil stood a few feet away, twirling the sword in his giant hands. It looked like a toy in his grip.

"What is the meaning of this? Remove your hand!" Sir Hugh said.

Sir Thomas spoke in a low voice. So low that Sir Hugh, Sir Basil, Quincy and I were the only ones to hear him.

"Know this," he said, the rage in his tone barely contained. "I will never see anything like this again. Am I clear? You will not come near my squire under any circumstances. If you do, if anything happens to him, if he is injured in any way and I find out you are the cause of it, I will strike you down myself. You will not harm this boy. Nod to show that you understand me."

Sir Hugh's face was as cold as stone and his eyes were full of poison. He looked at me and then at Sir Thomas and hissed, "You're a fool. I know, Sir Thomas. Don't think I don't. We both know who he is. You think you can protect him? Ha. I hardly think so."

Sir Thomas cocked his head, his eyes boring into Sir Hugh for the briefest of moments. I felt my stomach clench, momentarily forgetting the pain in my arm and shoulder, and suddenly found it difficult to breathe. What did Sir Hugh mean? He knew something about my past?

"You know nothing, Sir Hugh. Nothing at all. And let me be clear: this boy is now under my protection. I'm watching, Sir

Hugh. My men are watching. If anything happens to him, you'll be the first one I find." Sir Thomas' hand grasped hold of Sir Hugh's tunic and he pulled him just inches from his face. "Do you understand me?"

Sir Hugh's eyes narrowed. He didn't look frightened, but he knew that Sir Thomas, at least temporarily, had the upper hand. He barely nodded.

"Excellent," said Sir Thomas. "Now I am going to help you to your feet and Sir Basil is going to give you back your sword. You will take it and leave the field. If you ever raise it at Tristan again, you'd best next use it on yourself, for it will be the last act you perform on this earth. Do we have an understanding?"

Sir Hugh said nothing, only nodded briefly again. Sir Thomas stood and as he did so, pulled Sir Hugh to his feet. He brushed past Sir Thomas, grabbed his sword from Sir Basil and stormed off the field.

"Sergeanto, recommence with the training," said Sir Thomas. The squires immediately turned and began practicing as if nothing had happened.

"Tristan, are you hurt?" Sir Thomas asked.

"Not seriously, sire," I said. "I don't think anything is broken. It hurts quite a bit though."

Sir Thomas ran his hand along my shoulder and I winced. "It doesn't feel broken," he said.

"Tristan, I'm sorry. I didn't know what to do," Quincy said. He looked at me with downcast eyes as if he might break into tears at any moment.

"Not your fault, Quincy. You did nothing wrong. Don't give it another moment's thought," I said. He smiled at me in gratitude.

"That's right, Quincy. You are not to blame here. That lies squarely on the shoulders of Sir Hugh," Sir Basil said. He beamed at me. "Tristan, I saw what you did. Quick thinking."

"Sire, I am sorry to have caused any trouble . . . ," I said.

"Nonsense!" Sir Thomas interrupted. "I am glad that you are not seriously hurt, but I will want the physician to examine you. Sir Basil? Would you and Quincy excuse us for a moment?" he said.

Sir Basil nodded, and he and Quincy headed off the field.

"Tristan, tell me exactly what happened. I saw only the end," he said.

As we left the field, I recounted for him how Sir Hugh had found fault with my technique and tried to goad me into doing something that would give him a reason to attack me. When we passed by them, Sergeanto LeMaire and the other squires paused in their training and began clapping. A few whistles and "Hail Tristans!" could be heard.

"Good thing Sir Hugh wasn't here to see that," Sir Thomas said, laughing.

Good thing indeed. Sir Thomas turned as if to make his way back to the Commandery.

"Sire?"

"Yes?"

"What did Sir Hugh mean? When he said he knew who I was? And you said that I was now under your protection?"

Sir Thomas turned to look at me, with the usual smile on his face. But his eyes said something else. I wasn't sure what. They darted about, and for the first time since we had met, Sir Thomas didn't hold my gaze when he spoke.

"Tristan, Sir Hugh is an ass. I simply meant that as a knight I will defend and protect my squire from harm. Who knows what he thinks?"

I nodded, still unsure, standing in the dusty field thinking over what I had just witnessed. Sir Thomas turned to depart again, then stopped once more.

"Lad, though he is an arrogant fool, he's a dangerous man and never to be trusted. Never. I order you to stay out of his way. Do not approach Sir Hugh, ever, under any circumstances but especially alone. Is that clear?"

"Yes, sire," I said.

Sir Thomas left me then, and while I struggled to understand all that I had just witnessed, it was Sir Thomas' eyes that I kept seeing in my mind.

Eyes that told me much had been left unsaid.

On the Sea to Outremer
May 1191

fter the events on the practice field, Sir Thomas was suddenly less available, asking the sergeantos and even a few of the other knights to assist in my training. I suspected he was avoiding me, perhaps afraid that I would ask him more questions. And his manner when I did see and talk to him told me that the subject was closed. For the first few days, I thought of little else besides Sir Hugh's revelation (if that's what it was) but I finally realized that he was as Sir Thomas said: a fool. He probably knew nothing about me or my past and only wished to cruelly tempt me with knowledge he did not truly possess.

At any rate, the next few days were a flurry of activity and, as though he wished to keep me from wondering about Sir Hugh's actions, Sir Thomas piled on the work. Each morning the Master Sergeanto had an even lengthier list of duties for me, and between the chores and the training, I fell exhausted into my bed each night with little energy to think of anything but rest.

Three weeks later, six large Templar ships arrived in the port with returning Crusaders aboard. These were the vessels that would carry us to the Holy Land. The ships had been delayed in their voyage back from Outremer, and their arrival generated considerable excitement in the city. Crowds gathered at the waterfront to cheer. News from the Holy Land was eagerly debated and discussed. Apparently the Saladin was pressing outward from Jerusalem toward the coastal cities. I learned that our force would land near a city called Acre. From there we would try to push the Saladin back to the desert. King Richard was determined to drive the Saladin south and retake Jerusalem.

The King had departed Dover shortly after we had met with him that evening in the castle. According to Sir Thomas, he had left for London and his fleet would depart from Portsmouth on the southern coast. I had never been on board a ship or boat of any kind, and now I would be sailing across the sea as part of the King's fleet!

On the morning we left, Sir Thomas, Sir Basil and the entire regimento marched onto the docks. Not all of them would be leaving on the voyage. Some would remain behind to staff the Commandery, so good-byes were said all around.

Sir Hugh brushed past where I stood with Quincy and the other squires but did not glance in our direction. Walking briskly he stepped into a longboat, and its crew used the oars to slowly row it toward one of the ships lying anchored in the harbor.

Sir Thomas strode up to me. "Are you ready, lad?"

"Yes, sire," I said.

With that we climbed into another longboat. The crews rowed us out to our vessel, and I was relieved to see that Sir Hugh would be on a different ship. The boats pulled up to the sides of the ship where a large rope net had been dropped over the side. Everyone climbed up the netting and scampered aboard.

I found my spot belowdecks and laid my bedroll upon the small hammock where I would sleep. There wasn't much room. Bunks were built up and down the wall, little more than strands of rope, really, three beds high. I was happy to have the bottom. Our compartment was in the bow and the only light came from a few small slots that had been cut into the sides of the ship high above the waterline. It was dark and damp, and I would not recommend the smell. But I vowed to survive it for the next few weeks.

Wanting to see the sun again, I returned to the deck to find Sir Thomas standing at the rear section of the ship with Sir Basil. I climbed the small stairs that led to the quarterdeck and stood next to him.

"Sire, how long before we meet up with the King's fleet?" I asked.

"We rendezvous tomorrow morning in Portsmouth," he said.

"And once we're under way, how long until we reach Outremer?" I asked.

"It will depend on the wind. The fastest time I know of is two weeks. But I would say three weeks at least. Provided we encounter no problems," he said mischievously.

"Problems? What kind of problems?" I asked.

"Oh, the usual: storms, pirates, attacks by enemy fleets. Sea monsters have been known to slow us down occasionally," he said.

Pirates? Storms? Sea monsters? No one had spoken of these things before we left. Why had no one told me this?

Sir Thomas chuckled when he saw the look that crossed my face. "Rest easy, lad. We'll be fine," he said.

But I wasn't listening, as I was still considering pirates and sea monsters.

"Here it is, Tristan. Watch."

By then our ship had hoisted sail and cleared the harbor. Looking where Sir Thomas pointed, I could see the white cliffs of Dover behind us. I'd never before viewed anything so beautiful in my life. The chalk-white cliffs were bathed in the soft light of the sun. Rising up out of the ocean with no warning, it was as if God had reached down from heaven to pull the cleanest and purest part of the earth out of the ground for all to see. They towered over the city like a heavenly fortress, and I soon forgot all about pirates while I drank in the sight.

I watched the cliffs retreat from us as we turned south in the channel. Here the water was rougher, but the wind was stronger, and we picked up speed.

Shortly after daybreak we reached Portsmouth. There we were greeted by the King's fleet. The Lionheart's flagship sailed out of the harbor, leading a line of twenty vessels. His banner with the three golden lions on a crimson background was attached to the main mast, flapping proudly in the breeze.

At least that is what I was told. I saw none of it, for I lay in my hammock belowdecks, thrashing, vomiting and clutching my stomach, wishing that I were dead.

I've always been healthy and seldom caught the sicknesses or fevers that would strike the monks at the abbey. On that day, however, I believed that I was making up for it all. I had never felt so ill. Each movement of the ship sent my stomach reeling and rolled my eyes back in my head. I lay in the swinging hammock promising to do anything God asked if he would just make the ship stop moving up and down and side to side.

It was Quincy who told me of the rendezvous and the impressive array of ships that now sailed toward Outremer. The motion of the ship didn't seem to bother him at all. He visited me often in the hold, where I could scarcely lift my head, keeping me apprised of events as they happened on the ship.

Finally, on the third day, my stomach settled somewhat and I made my way to the deck, squinting in the sun like a mole. As the deck heaved to and fro, I thought I would be sick again. I held fast to the deck railing until the wave of nausea passed. It felt good to breathe in the fresh air. The life of a sailor was definitely not for me.

Sir Thomas found me on the deck, desperately clutching the railing.

"Feeling better?" he asked.

"I'll be happy to never sail again," I said.

"Ha. Be glad we're not taking the land route. It takes months. Riding along, choking in the dust, burning in the sun, freezing in the rain. Saddle sores. Believe me, this is much better," he said.

"If you say so, sire," I answered, still feeling miserable. Sir Thomas chuckled again at my discomfort and moved off.

Most of the time on the ship I was bored beyond belief. We were often out of sight of land, with nothing to look at but water. And more water. There was little to do except sleep and pace about the deck. Some days I even took a turn at the oars just to have something to do.

Once in the Mediterranean the wind was stronger and the ship moved over the water at a quicker pace. Passing through the Strait of Gibraltar I saw the mighty rock that had guarded the passage since time began. A few days past the rock, we sailed around the Isle of Cyprus, not stopping, for the King wished to reach Acre as soon as possible.

Three weeks to the day after leaving Dover, the ships made landfall a day's ride to the west of Acre, at a spot where the coast leveled out to form a natural harbor. We had to swim the horses to shore, and it took two full days to move all of the cargo and supplies off the ships. My legs felt as if they were made of stone columns when I first stepped on land after nearly three weeks at sea. I wanted to kiss the ground, but merely rejoiced that it didn't move as I walked upon it.

I wasn't sure what I had expected of Outremer, but the land surprised me. Having heard the knights speak of the arid desert, I was surprised to find the coastal area, although rocky, to be full of green trees and shrubs. The climate was warmer than England to be sure, but in many ways it reminded me of Dover, except here the cliffs were made of rock, not chalk.

We made camp right on the sand. Within a day, the beach became a city of campaign tents, each one flying a regimento or battle flag. Large cook fires were built, and as we sat around them at night, I loved watching the embers rise high into the sky. It was as if each one carried a message to heaven. The Templars conducted mass by firelight and passed the hours in song and storytelling while we waited for orders to march.

The King's headquarters tent was not more than a few yards away from where I slept. Now and then I would see him outside his tent, at a table holding maps and other documents. He spent hours in consultation with his military advisers. Plans were being made and battle orders drawn. Word passed through the camp that Saracens were near.

We spent the next week organizing, resting and preparing to move toward Acre. When the horses had rested and regained their land legs, the call came to move out. Quincy and I went with the other squires to retrieve our knights' horses from where they were hobbled on the shore. Quincy seemed calm, whistling quietly to himself as we gathered up the saddles and halters.

"Aren't you nervous?" I asked.

"What? Nervous? Why? Oh yes. This is your first time in enemy territory. You get used to it," he said.

"Really?" I couldn't imagine that.

"Oh sure. You'll see. The knights are well trained. They know what they're doing all right. It'll be fine," he said, smiling. But his confidence was not contagious. I still felt on edge.

I had Dauntless saddled and prepared to go when Sir Thomas found me. His chain mail had been polished to a high sheen, and there in the sun I helped dress him. When he was properly outfitted, he mounted the horse. He took the battle sword from me and buckled it securely around his waist. I handed him his iron-tipped lance, hoping he wouldn't notice my shaking hands. He settled himself into the saddle, stood up and down in the stirrups a few times to find a comfortable spot, then sat still.

"Are you ready?" he asked me.

No! I wasn't ready for anything other than perhaps getting on board the ship and sailing back to England.

"Yes, sire," I said.

"Are you afraid?" he asked.

In truth I was terrified. My hands quivered as I attended to my duties, and my breath came in small gasps. It felt as if I couldn't get enough air in my lungs. My vision began to close in. I was in no way prepared for this. Everything that had come before—the training, the practice, the days in the Commandery—was as faint as a dream. However, I could not, must not, let Sir Thomas feel that he had made a choice unworthy of him.

"A little," I answered.

"That's good, Tristan. If you had told me you were not afraid, I wouldn't have believed you. The important thing is to stay alert at all times. Here in Outremer, battles tend to happen quickly and with little warning. Keep your eyes open. If a fight starts, stay focused on your duties. We've practiced and discussed it many times. The most common thing is that I'll lose my lance or it will break. Stay near the quartermaster, and if you see me riding back, ride forward with a replacement. You'll do fine. We may not even engage the enemy. Our scouts have seen Saracen patrols, but have not yet encountered a large force. We might march to Acre unopposed," he said.

For some reason, I very much doubted that. Something told me I would see my first action very soon. Death was coming. The air had changed. We were in an alien land, marching forward as intruders, and everything felt upside down and out of place.

An order was shouted to march. The knights and men-at-arms moved out four abreast. They left the beach encampment, moving inland toward the higher ground rising east along the shore. The sergeantos and squires came behind the knights. I rode a sorrel mare and Quincy rode along beside me. A leather holster was attached to my saddle, and in it I placed an extra lance for Sir Thomas.

"Are you still nervous?" Quincy asked.

"Not at all. At St. Alban's we had to fight off invading monasteries quite frequently. Compared with hordes of marauding Benedictines, this is nothing."

Quincy stared at me, his brows knitted.

"It's a joke. Knowing I may be marching toward my death tends to make me nervous," I said.

Quincy chuckled at my discomfort. "I can tell you that most of the time nothing happens. We spend more time riding than fighting. And we don't see much from back here."

To calm myself, I tried passing the time by counting the size of our force. Though it was hard to get an accurate count with everyone stretched out in the column, I counted twelve Templar flags. With each regimento about seventy knights strong, plus men-at-arms, sergeantos and squires, I made our numbers to be nearly two thousand men. This of course included the non-Templar forces of the King's Guards. If we ran into opposition, I hoped it was enough. I knew that Templars never left the field of battle unless outnumbered by more than three to one. The thought of facing a force of six thousand Saracens terrified me.

We rode along for hours, stopping now and then to rest and water the horses. In the afternoon as we crested a small ridge, the order came to halt. There was confusion at the front of the column, orders were shouted and trumpets called. In the noise and disarray I made out one word that sent my heart leaping to my throat.

Saracens!

Outremer, the Holy Land

13

I quickly learned that war is mostly organized chaos and that as Sir Thomas said, it often happens without warning.

In the valley below us there stood a large advance force of Saracens. Seeing them for the first time did nothing to quell the fear within me. They looked formidable and ready to fight. At first glance, their lines appeared to stretch out for miles. I struggled to take it all in. They began waving their brightly colored battle flags back and forth. Unlike our traditional flags, they held banners that hung vertically from tall poles raised high by a mounted carrier. I quickly counted them and estimated their numbers were nearly equal to our own. It was as if they appeared by magic. Surely our scouts and mounted patrols must have noticed them ahead of us. But from where I rode, I got the feeling that we had stumbled across them unexpectedly.

As they spread out across the valley floor I saw a sea of turbans, mostly white, but here and there I noticed some were striped with different colors; greens and blacks.

"Why do those Saracens have striped turbans?" I asked Quincy over the gathering noise of our deployment.

"Those are their commanders. They direct the fighting and give orders to the individual squads," he answered. Somewhere from their lines a trumpet sounded and their cavalry began moving into position.

Their horses were magnificent; tall, stately mounts that were draped from head to flanks in brightly colored blankets, some of which completely covered the horse's head with holes cut out for the eyes. Many of the coverings were decorated with stars and other designs.

"Why do they cover their horses so?"

"Sir Basil says it's to protect the horses from the sun when they ride through the desert. They are quite beautiful though, aren't they?" Quincy asked.

Their horsemen carried shields and scimitars, not lances. I wondered at this, since it seemed that the longer lance would give our knights an advantage, but perhaps the shields countered their effectiveness.

Turning from the mounted warriors I studied their foot soldiers more closely. They were dressed in simple tunics, most of them white or light brown. All of them carried scimitars. Their scabbards were looped around the neck and shoulders, not carried at the belt, probably because the weapons were so heavy. Here and there I saw that a few men wore iron guards to protect their arms but I did not see any mail or armor among them.

Despite this surprise our forces moved rapidly to form a line along the ridge. The King and his guards took the center. I saw Sir Thomas move to the King's left with about thirty mounted Templars. Sir Basil took the right with about the same number. Other regimentos followed until they had fully deployed along the rise.

The men-at-arms dismounted, leaving their horses with the sergeantos in the rear. They were trained to fight on foot and would charge forward in an attempt to break the enemy lines. Taking their place in front of the King, they lined up three deep with swords drawn and shields at the ready. To me it looked like everyone was running about in confusion, but before I knew it all the forces had deployed along the ridge and were ready to attack.

Down below, the Saracens scurried about, moving their men and horses into position. Buglers at the rear of their columns raised extremely long, straight horns, roughly the length of a man, and sounded their call to arms. They began to deploy in nearly the same fashion as we did, perhaps four or five hundred yards away. As they made ready to attack, they began to shout *"Allah Akbar"* over and over again.

"Quincy! What is that chanting?" I shouted.

"It's their battle cry. It means 'God is great!'"

As if to answer the chants of the Saracens, the knights began singing from the Psalm of David: "Not unto us, O Lord, not unto us, but to your name give glory!"

"Watch!" Quincy shouted over the din. "After they sing the Psalm, they'll order a charge!"

Then I heard the sound of our trumpets, and the battle was on.

My horse began to fuss when the noise and shouting started. I reached forward to quiet her with a pat on her neck. We squires strained our eyes to keep track of our knights as they rode forward. I heard the Templars shout *"Beauseant!"* over the noise. It was a Templar war cry and it meant "Be glorious!" Sir Thomas and the other knights around him lowered their lances, surging forward as one. Their horses charged across the rocky ground, and the noise even from a distance was deafening.

The King and his guard did not charge, holding their position on the ridge, watching as first the knights, then the men-at-arms plowed forth. The Saracens, to their credit, did not give ground easily. Countering the charge, their horsemen rode straight at the knights with scimitars held high. The first wave of Saracens and knights collided with a tremendous clang as steel met steel. Horses reared and men screamed and the dust flew. I lost sight of Sir Thomas in the mass of bodies and swirling clouds of dust that squirmed in the valley below.

As I glanced again at the King astride his white warhorse, I noticed to my disgust Sir Hugh sitting next to him on horseback. He carried no lance, content to watch the conflict from the safety of the ridge. Studying the battle below, I was desperate for a sign of Sir Thomas. For a moment I considered spurring my horse forward, but fear held me in place. My grip tightened on the reins and I felt paralyzed, unable to move or speak.

Without warning the battle began to turn against us. Some of the men-at-arms broke ranks, sprinting back toward our lines at the top of the ridge. I heard the shouts of King Richard and his advisers, exhorting them to return and face the enemy. The King spurred his warhorse down the hill and met the first wave of retreating men. Waving his sword he shouted, but his words were lost in the noise and distance. It did have an effect on the men though. For a moment they stopped running and rallied.

An order was given from somewhere, and the sergeantos, who had been held in reserve, left us behind as they rode down the hill into the fight. The dust was worse than ever and made it almost impossible to see. But I could tell we were losing ground.

King Richard was not yet in the thick of the fighting but close, as he pleaded with his forces to fight on. With no concern for his own safety he spurred his horse farther into the mass of teeming bodies.

Just then, the Lionheart's horse reared up and he was thrown to the ground. He staggered to his feet still holding the reins, but his horse was wild with fright and tore out of the King's grasp, running toward the ridgetop. King Richard's rash act had surprised his guard and he had left them behind. Now the men abandoning the fight had obscured their view of the King. For the moment, no one noticed him standing in the dust defenseless. A stream of panicked men ran around him with the Saracens fast behind them.

"Quincy, the King!" I shouted, pointing to where Richard now stood with a line of Saracens not more than a few yards away. The knights were fighting valiantly, but were still losing ground. The King waited with his sword at the ready, picking up a shield that had been dropped by a retreating soldier.

Without thinking, I spurred my horse and pointed it toward the King. I had no plan in mind other than to get between the King and the attacking force.

A few scattered men ran past me, but the fighting had slowed at the base of the ridge. I saw a Saracen run at King Richard with his scimitar held high. King Richard stepped aside, thrusting his sword into the side of the man attacking him.

In a few more seconds I reined my horse up beside the King and jumped from the saddle.

"Your majesty! You are in danger! Take this horse to safety!" I yelled.

The King parried another blow from a Saracen, and I pulled my short sword and took after the man myself, swinging it wildly as hard as I could and screaming at the top of my lungs. The man stopped and stared at me, easily blocking blow after blow. Then for some unexplainable reason he turned and ran.

The King looked at me, but didn't speak.

"Please, your highness! You must take my horse!" I said.

Grabbing the reins, King Richard quickly mounted up. I watched him weave his way through the mass of men, heading back up the ridge.

All around me was confusion. I heard shouts and grunts and groans of agony. I heard men calling out for God and the shrieks of the dying. Looking over my shoulder, I saw that many of our men-at-arms were again in full retreat up the face of the ridge. If something didn't break our way soon, we would be driven from the field entirely.

I spotted a Templar banner clutched in the hands of a sergeanto, who lay dead on the ground. Not stopping to think, I grabbed it from his hands and raised it high over my head. Waving it back and forth I hollered, "Beauseant! Beauseant!" as loudly as I could.

At first, my shouts had no effect. Then I heard a few men nearby begin to join in, yelling at the top of their lungs. Soon a few more took up the cheer. All along the ridge where our men-at-arms had been falling back, they stopped and looked down at us on the floor of the small valley. I yelled louder, so loudly I thought my throat might catch fire. Slowly the men who had been running away stopped. With a mighty roar they came charging back into the fight.

Seconds later a river of men rushed past me, many of them cut, bleeding or limping from various wounds, but run they did.

They crashed back into the Saracen lines, screaming and yelling and shrieking for their lives.

I found myself inside a swirling tide of butchery. I heard shrieks of agony as bodies slammed into one another. I learned firsthand the sound a bone makes when it is broken by a sword. I came to recognize the horrible ripping sound that flesh makes when it is pierced by a lance.

All around me, men fought like desperate, cornered animals. Some had no swords or shields at all and merely grappled in the dirt, digging at each other's eyes, biting fingers and pulling hair. I saw a sergeanto with no weapon save his helmet, which he had removed from his head, swinging it wildly back and forth, knocking several men unconscious until he himself was overcome by three Saracens.

I held fast to the banner, brandishing it before me, yelling encouragement to the men until my throat was raw. My arms began to throb from holding the flag and swinging my sword. After a while, perhaps from fatigue, it felt as if time had slowed and the noise and confusion of the battle around me took on a curious stillness. It was as if I saw everything in slow motion. I felt dizzy and light-headed but knew instinctively that I must keep the banner held high and my sword in my hand if I was to remain alive.

Finally, the enemy lines were broken. Soon our men were chasing them across the field in the other direction. In a few more minutes it was over. The Saracens were completely routed, sounding a retreat and running east. The knights and men-at-arms gave a mighty shout. Slowly the dust settled and the horses quieted. All that was left was the carnage around me.

The ground was littered with bodies. From where I stood I could barely tell who was friend and who was foe. In truth it did not really matter, for all of them were dead, dying or severely wounded. The sounds of battle were quickly replaced with cries for mercy and prayers to both God and Allah to end their suffering. The sight of it made me weak, and it took all my concentration not to keel over in the dirt. I looked everywhere for Sir Thomas and soon found him, kneeling beside an injured Saracen, offering him water. Sir Basil was also helping tend the wounded. A great sense of relief came over me that they were both still alive.

I felt sick from the carnage and bloodshed around me. Wounded men, now missing limbs, screamed in misery. Some crawled on their hands and knees, pushing themselves through the dirt, pleading for someone to help them. I closed my eyes to the horror.

Looking up the ridge I could see King Richard, now remounted on his warhorse, his banner flapping strongly in the breeze. He surveyed the field and raised his sword in triumph. I looked again at the field scattered with bodies and dying men. My sword was somehow still in my hand, and I was shocked to see bloodstains upon it. I had no memory of how they had gotten there.

A few moments later Quincy rode up and dismounted, his voice full of excitement.

"Tristan! I saw what you did for the King. All the squires are talking about it! You're a hero! Wasn't our victory glorious?" he asked excitedly.

It didn't feel glorious. It didn't feel glorious at all.

THE CITY OF ACRE, OUTREMER
JUNE 1191

14

We spent that night camped right on the battlefield. I was exhausted, but the aftermath of our victory meant only more work. Everyone, even the knights, pitched in to carry casualties from the field. The physicians worked like demons long into the night, treating the injured. Burial details were formed and prayers were said over the simple graves of our fallen comrades.

The battle had been won, but I couldn't shake the feeling that the cost had been too great. We had lost nearly one hundred men, and almost double that had been wounded in some manner.

When I finally had a moment to catch my breath, I dropped to the ground near a cook fire, but found I had no appetite. A pot of stew simmered on the coals, but the very thought of food made me ill. I sat staring off at nothing.

Sensing movement, I looked up to see Sir Thomas standing beside me. I should have stood, but I was too tired.

"I've just come from a conference with the King," he said.

"Yes, sire?" Uh-oh.

"He tells me a certain squire rode to his rescue at a critical point in the fight this afternoon."

From his tone I couldn't tell if he was angry or proud.

"He did?"

"Yes. Apparently this squire gave up his horse so the King could return to safety."

I shrugged, staring at the fire.

"Tristan, what you did was incredibly brave. And also dangerous. I believe I left you with orders to stay at your post unless I required your assistance during the fighting."

I looked up at Sir Thomas and saw the concerned smile on his face. He wasn't mad exactly.

"Forgive me, sire, I don't know what came over me. When I saw the King there with the Saracens about to overtake him, I . . . well . . . I just reacted," I stammered.

"I understand. And you've become quite the hero to the entire army. You saved a comrade without thinking of yourself, and the King, no less. That is one of the marks of greatness in a warrior, Tristan. But please. No more such acts of bravery. England can always get a new King. Good squires are not easy for me to find," he said.

I looked at Sir Thomas and he winked at me.

"Get some rest," he said. "We ride out in the morning."

It felt good to receive his praise, but in truth Sir Thomas' words did little to resolve the conflicting emotions that poured through me. I struggled to understand what I had seen that day, and more important why any of it had happened in the first place. Finally, exhaustion overcame me, and I slept right there by the fire.

The next afternoon our forces rode onto the plains surrounding the city of Acre and relieved a large force of Crusaders that had besieged it some months earlier. It was a beautiful spot, sitting right on the seacoast. From our position I could hear the waves crashing against the rocks below, and the sound was almost comforting somehow. The city itself sat on a promontory that jutted out into the sea. Out in the harbor, several Crusader ships bobbed in the waves as they blockaded the port. Beyond the stone walls, I could see the tiled rooftops of the buildings inside and as we moved into position the Saracens began to yell and jeer at us from the battlements, but they soon lost interest and fell silent.

"It's a pretty spot," I said to Quincy as we surveyed the countryside.

"Yes, it is. Sir Basil was here years ago. He says it was quite a wild place then. There are caves below the city, and I guess many pirates and marauders used them as a base. Perhaps we'll have a chance to explore them someday," he said.

I would rather have left the caves to the pirates. I much preferred the open air. And who knew? There could still be pirates hiding in them. I'd never met any, but I was fairly certain I wasn't going to like pirates, just on principle.

The garrison of Saracens inside Acre had been holding out for months, desperate for the Saladin to send reinforcements, which he had yet to do. Upon his arrival, King Richard met with the Saracen leaders under a flag of truce and immediately demanded they cede the city to his command. They refused.

For six weeks we camped outside the city, fighting sporadically but mainly waiting for them to just give up. Exhausted and running low on food, they were overwhelmed with sick and wounded and could barely mount a defense. The King preferred to wait them out, not wanting to needlessly sacrifice men in an assault when it seemed likely they would capitulate before long.

Their surrender finally came on the eleventh of July and Acre was ours. We marched inside the gates, and I watched the Saracens, now prisoners of war, being led away.

The Christian citizens of Acre were overjoyed to have the city under the Crusaders' control once again. They had been well treated during the Saladin's occupation. He had issued proclamations allowing them to worship as they pleased and to keep their homes and businesses. But when the siege began, not only was the city surrounded, but the Crusaders had closed off the port as well, and no supplies at all could get in or out. With no medicines and very little food the people had grown sick and hungry.

The King immediately sent word to Cyprus and points east, and in a few days' time ships began arriving with food and medicines. The Templar physicians enlisted the aid of us squires to help them treat the sick, and we shared our food with some who were near starvation. In these days the true character of men like Sir Thomas, Sir Basil and Quincy and the other Templars was revealed to me. They were not just there to fight for fighting's sake. Their purpose was the liberation of their fellow Christians.

The first days of our reoccupation, when I wasn't attending to my duties, I took what time I could to explore the city. As in Dover, a marketplace took up the center of the city with stone paved streets leading in and out of it in all four directions. Every building was constructed of stone with brightly colored awnings covering the doorways and windows. It was a marked contrast as all of Dover's buildings were built of timber and though it had been a noisy, lively place, Acre felt more subdued and quieter. Perhaps the long siege had taken some of the spirit out of the people.

Being inside Acre confirmed what I'd felt as we had ridden out from the beach upon first landing here; that I was in an alien place. Everything from the spicy smells of the cooking fires to the elegant archways of the buildings and temples was new and unusual. It was going to take some getting used to.

Sir Thomas and I moved our belongings into rooms in the Knights' Hall. Unlike Dover, where the squires had slept in separate quarters, knights and squires shared rooms. Our days quickly assumed a routine similar to life at the Dover Commandery. We attended to our horses and equipment, and worked on preparing the city's defenses. Though we had broken and beaten a Saracen force on our way into the city, no one expected the Saladin to give up easily.

"This defeat won't sit well with the Saladin," Sir Thomas said as we walked along a parapet above the east wall. "He'll be back soon, and we'll likely be on the other end of a siege."

Sir Thomas was possessed of an uncommon energy in those days. He was everywhere at once. I was amazed at the depth and array of his knowledge of battle tactics. I learned much just by watching him. No detail was too small. He would climb high in the towers and along the battlements that lined the city walls, looking for weaknesses. He constantly checked the sight lines of the archers and made sure that each siege engine or ballistae—the large mechanical crossbows that threw giant arrows at the enemy—was placed in the most strategic position. He was fanatical about making sure our positions were as well defended as possible.

Each day, thoughts of what I had seen on the battlefield paraded through my mind. I wondered how Sir Thomas was able to dedicate himself to a life like this. How could a man accept such horror and carnage and not be affected by what he saw?

One morning as we finished our inspection of the northern battlements, I couldn't keep my questions to myself any longer.

"Sire, forgive me, but I am troubled by something," I said.

"I could tell. You haven't been yourself the past few days. Tell me what it is," he said.

"It is the battle, sire, what I saw, what we did . . ." I couldn't find the words.

"You have a good heart, Tristan. I could tell it bothered you. It should. It was horrible," he said.

"So why do we fight, then, if it is such a terrible thing?" I asked.

"That's a good question, Tristan. A warrior, a true warrior, must always ask if his cause is just. The taking of another's life is not a trifle. You fight because you must. There can be no other option," he said.

"But sire, why do we fight *here*?" I asked. "What is wrong with talking and sorting out our differences?"

"The fighting usually starts when the talking ends. It lasts until men grow weary of the fighting and seek to talk again. Then the fighting stops . . . for a while. But in the end there is always more fighting. It is what men do. It has always been this way. So if we fight, we must choose *why* we fight. Then we fight with honor. It is the only way. It will take time, and I'm afraid you may see many more horrible things before you do, but you will understand eventually," he said.

I was still confused, but as I worked things out in my mind, I kept seeing certain images over and over. It was the sight of Sir Thomas after the battle giving water to a fallen enemy. I thought of Sir Basil carrying a wounded man from the field. I remembered the Templar physicians treating both sick Christian and Muslim children in the city. If I was going to fight, I would fight nobly and with honor, like Sir Thomas and his comrades.

For weeks, we worked long, hard hours, rising before the sun came up and falling dead tired into our beds at night. One morning there was word that King Richard and his guards would be leaving the next day. He would ride east to inspect his forces in Tyre, another coastal city. The King desperately wanted to take the Crusaders who were waiting in Tyre and press toward Jerusalem in the south, not be cooped up in Acre if the Saladin's armies returned and surrounded the city.

I was working in the stable when word came that Sir Thomas wished to see me. I found him in the main room of the Knights' Hall, seated at one of the long tables with Sir Basil.

"Ah, Tristan, there you are," he said.

"Yes, sire. You wished to see me?"

"Yes, I did. You have no doubt heard that King Richard will be departing shortly?" he asked.

"Yes, sire," I said.

Reaching into his tunic he removed a letter and handed it to me. It was thick and felt as if it had something inside it other than just sheets of parchment. It was sealed with Sir Thomas' mark in wax.

"I need you to take this letter to one of the King's Guards. He will be somewhere in the Crusaders' Palace. His name is Gaston. A rather burly fellow. Brown hair. Give the letter to him, and only him. It is for the Master of the Order in London, and Gaston will see that it gets to him safely. Do you understand?"

"Yes, sire. Gaston of the King's Guards," I repeated.

"Excellent. Now off with you," he said.

I left the Knights' Hall and in a few minutes reached the Crusaders' Palace. Asking around, I was told that Gaston might be found in the stables below the palace. Finding my way there, I walked toward a large open doorway that led inside. The stables were quiet and nearly deserted, save for a solitary guard who sat on a barrel in front of one of the stalls, sharpening a small dagger with a stone. At my approach he stood, sheathing the dagger, and rested his forearm on the hilt of his sword.

His casual stance jogged something in my memory.

It was possible I had seen him here in Acre, passing by the barracks or perhaps on duty outside the King's quarters. But he seemed more familiar than that. As I drew closer, it came to me. I *had* seen him before. Not here in Acre, but before that, in the streets of Dover.

On the day I had been followed as I led Dauntless to Little John's smithy, this man was the guard who entered the tavern and, I was willing to wager, sent the two drunks after me. What's more, I saw in his face that he recognized me as well, though he tried not to show it.

"Do I know you?" I asked.

The guard shook his head. "No. I don't think so. State your business."

"I'm looking for someone. I was told he'd be here," I said.

He shrugged. Then he stared off over my shoulder.

"Have you ever been to Dover?" I asked.

"No," he said. But he fidgeted nervously.

"You followed me a few months ago. You stood outside the Whistling Pig Tavern and watched while two drunks tried to beat me and steal my knight's horse," I said.

The man looked down at the ground, then up at the ceiling—everywhere but at my face.

"I don't know what you're talking about. I haven't been posted in Dover in years. You shouldn't be making such rash accusations, boy," he said, finally looking at me. His tone had changed, full of menace now. "I would learn to keep my mouth shut if I were you, squire. Now, run along."

"I want to know why you—" But I couldn't get the words out, because before I knew it he had pushed me roughly to the ground. I sprawled in the dirt, stunned, and watched his hand move back to the hilt of his sword.

"I have no time for this, boy. Leave. Before I teach you a lesson in manners you'll not soon forget." He glared down at me. I stood up, never taking my eyes off him.

"You'll answer for this," I said. "Sir Thomas and the Templars will—"

He moved to pull the sword, but not quickly, believing that he could easily frighten me. I was faster. I grabbed his arm and held on to it with all my strength. I pushed him back against the door to the stall, pinning him in place.

"You fool!" he said as he struggled. "Attacking a King's Guard? You'll be hanged!"

"Perhaps, but not before you give me some answers. Why did you follow me that day? Why did you send those men after me?!"

The man said nothing, only attempted to free his arm from my grip. Just as he was about to break loose, someone spoke from behind us.

"What is the meaning of this?" Before I could turn, I saw the guard's eyes widen in fear. Though I had heard it up close only a few times, I recognized the voice. I released my grip on the guard and spun around. The Lionheart stood before me. He had a small squad of guards with him, two of whom had drawn their swords and now pointed them at me. He was dressed to ride, wearing his red tunic with the golden lions emblazoned on his chest, leather riding pants and knee-high boots. A large sword hung at his belt, and he held a helmet under his arm.

I was in trouble if I did not act carefully.

"Your highness," I said, bowing.

King Richard stared at me and a slow look of recognition came over his face.

"You are that boy, Thomas Leux's squire?" he asked.

"Yes, your majesty," I said.

"You came to my aid on the battlefield," he said. It was not a question, more a statement of fact.

I shrugged.

"Why are you assaulting one of my guards?" he asked.

"I'm afraid it was a misunderstanding. I was looking for someone. Sir Thomas sent me with a message for one of your men. This man and I got into an argument—"

The King waved his hand and his two guards sheathed their weapons.

"I take offense at those who would attack my men," he said. "I could have you hanged."

Something told me to be bold. For some reason, being in my presence made the King uneasy. Still, he was the monarch. He could end my life with a word. But I felt he would respect me more if I showed no fear.

"You could, sire," I said. "My apologies." I bowed again slightly, but held his gaze.

His eyes bored into me again, much as they had that night in the castle at Dover. I tried not to act nervous or afraid, but I was in over my head, and his stare began to make me uncomfortable. It was almost like he was trying to decide: Should I kill this boy? Or knight him?

"I owe a great debt to Sir Thomas, and since you intervened on my behalf in battle, I will overlook this offense. Do not let it happen again. Never threaten one of my men. Understood?"

"Yes, your majesty," I said, bowing again.

"Who is it you seek?" he asked.

I told him that I had a message for a guard named Gaston. King Richard barked a command and one of the guards stepped forward. The King brushed past me into the stables, and the rest of his squad followed as they readied their mounts to depart.

I stared after the man I'd just tussled with, but he ignored me as he went to the stall where his horse was quartered and began adjusting the saddle.

Gaston stood before me, a dour-looking fellow, but he matched the description Sir Thomas had given me.

"Sir Thomas asked me to give this to you," I said, handing him the letter. "It is for the Master of the Order. Can you see it safely to London?"

"Of course. I know Sir Thomas well. After I ride with the King to Tyre, I'll be posted back to England. I'll make sure the letter reaches the Master," Gaston replied.

I thought it best to get away from the King as soon as possible so I quickly left the palace grounds. I walked across the city square, climbing up on the parapets over the main gate. A few moments later the King and his guards departed the city to the east. I watched as the Lionheart rode out surrounded by his men, back astride his pure white warhorse. I kept my eyes on them until they disappeared from sight on the eastern horizon.

My duty done, I left the parapet intending to return to the Knights' Hall, where I still had unfinished work. As I made my way through the busy streets, I could suddenly hear them far off in the distance. The sound of Saracen trumpets.

The Saladin was coming.

15

he Saladin returned to Acre with a vengeance. The trumpets first sounded that morning, and his forces had encircled the city by nightfall. Atop the walls we watched his army deploy in wave after wave. I couldn't even begin to count the number of battle flags and had no idea how many men he had brought to bear on Acre, but it easily numbered in the thousands.

When we had taken Acre, the port had been reopened and supply ships from Cyprus and other points east had arrived almost daily. We had been able to build up all the stores and had dug numerous new wells. Now we were garrisoned in a fortress city, well supplied with food and water, but I felt a mild sense of panic as I watched the Saracens surround us. How would we defeat such a large force, cooped up as we were with no room to maneuver or counterattack?

Sir Thomas pointed to a large tent that was pitched on a rise to the east several hundred yards away, out of range of our ballistae and siege engines.

"That is the Saladin's command tent. He'll be directing the siege himself," Sir Thomas said. I kept watch on the tent whenever there was a spare moment but could not tell if one of the tiny figures I saw moving about was the Saladin.

"Sire, surrounded like this, locked in, what will we do?" I asked, unable to keep the nervousness and fear from creeping into my voice.

"We fight. We never stop fighting, Tristan. Rest easy, lad. We're well dug in here. Acre will not be an easy plum for the Saladin to pick," Sir Thomas said.

"Yes, sire," I said. Sir Thomas smiled and left the parapet, no doubt needing to confer with the other knights to begin planning the defense of the city. I continued watching as the forces below us filed forward, pitching their campaign tents and beginning their preparations for battle. Though I desperately wanted to believe Sir Thomas, I found it hard to share his confidence.

The first attack did not come until three days later. The Saladin began with a flurry of flaming arrows shot over the city walls in an attempt to set fire to the buildings inside. Because most of the structures were made of stone, this had little effect. A few wagons hit by stray arrows caught fire, but there was minimal damage. We returned fire with our own siege engines, hurling boulders and pots of flaming pitch at their lines. A few tents caught fire, but I don't believe any Saracens were seriously injured.

For the next two weeks, it became a game of feint, thrust and retreat between our fighters inside the city and the Saracens outside the walls. They probed and prodded our defenses, searching for a weakness. I was grateful Sir Thomas had been so diligent in preparing the city for the Saladin's return. He tried to keep things normal, insisting that we squires continue our training with the sword and making sure that we kept all the knights' equipment in fighting shape.

Some knights thought that perhaps the Saladin intended to try to starve us out. That he was content to wait until our garrison had run out of supplies. But other knights disagreed, believing that the Saladin was waiting for even more reinforcements to arrive. Then he would throw his men against the walls until we were overwhelmed by the sheer weight of numbers. Though we were hard to get at inside the city, the Saladin's army was now more than three times the size of the fighting force inside Acre.

As the days passed, Sir Thomas never let up in his furious level of activity. He walked among the battlements atop the wall, encouraging the men who stood guard. From immediately after morning mass to well after evening prayers Sir Thomas could be found inspecting the parapets or drilling the archers and men-at-arms. He never stopped moving, thinking or planning.

Sir Hugh, on the other hand, was hardly seen at all once the Saladin had arrived. After days of waiting for something significant to happen, Quincy and I stood one morning atop the eastern wall of the city watching the activity of the forces on the plains below, discussing where Sir Hugh might have disappeared to.

"He's slithered away like the worm he is," Quincy said. And he suddenly dropped to the ground, flopping about.

"Sir Hugh is the regimental worm!" he said, laughing. "He's found himself a pile of dung to dig through and . . ."

I began to laugh as well, but was startled by a hand upon my shoulder and turned to see Sir Thomas standing behind me. Quincy heard my gasp and jumped to his feet, embarrassed to be caught fooling around. He nervously brushed the dust from his tunic.

"Quincy, are you ill?" he asked.

"No, sire, I feel fine," Quincy replied.

"Hmm. With your flopping around like that, I thought perhaps you might have caught some sort of fever," he said.

Quincy looked stricken, unable to tell from Sir Thomas' expression whether or not he was in serious trouble.

I tried to save him.

"Um. Sire. Well. Quincy was explaining to me, uh . . . about a new method of sword fighting . . . ," I stammered.

Sir Thomas raised an eyebrow. "Sword fighting? Really? A new technique that requires one to rest on one's back, squirming in the dirt?"

"Yes, sire, yes, you see, we saw one of the King's Guards demonstrating it a few weeks ago. Apparently it originated in Spain. If you stumble or fall during battle, you're still able to defend yourself from the ground. And Quincy was demonstrating . . ."

Sir Thomas interrupted me. "Yes, well, I admire your initiative in studying a new *technique*," he said. "However, I think there is perhaps more important work to be done. If you have no duties to attend to, I can perhaps ask the Master Sergeanto to . . ."

"No need, sire," I interrupted. "We were just preparing to leave for the stable to tend the horses. And after that I'll be polishing your chain mail, sire, polishing it to a high sheen. Yes, sire. We wouldn't want the ocean air to cause rust."

"Very well . . ."

Before Sir Thomas could finish, a shout went up from the Saladin's lines. It was after their morning prayers, and from down below we began to hear chants of "Allah Akhbar." Sir Thomas stepped quickly to the edge of the parapet, his eyes sweeping the field.

"Tristan, step quickly to the Knights' Hall and bring my sword and mail. Quincy, find Sir Basil and have him alert the other knights. Hurry!"

"Sir Thomas, what is happening?" I asked.

"They are preparing to attack, Tristan. Any moment now. Be quick and fetch my equipment. Now go!"

As Quincy and I rushed down the steps, I could hear Sir Thomas shouting commands and instructions to the men-at-arms and sounding the call to arms. The urgency in Sir Thomas' voice told me that this was something different, unlike the attacks we'd faced so far. My stomach lurched, and I was reminded of how I'd felt riding into that first battle so many weeks ago. I began to feel light-headed as I ran, and it became difficult to raise and lower my feet, as if the ground had turned to mud. I tried to push the nervousness down and focus on my duties, but images of the carnage in the valley flashed through my mind, and I felt myself growing afraid. I tried to pray but found myself unable to.

In a few moments what had been a relatively quiet morning inside the city became a whirlwind of activity. Quincy left me on the run to locate Sir Basil as I raced through the streets to the Knights' Hall, where I retrieved Sir Thomas' gear.

I retraced my steps and found Sir Thomas on the parapet shouting out orders. Peering over at the Saladin's army I saw a flurry of activity out on the plains. Everything seemed to be happening in slow motion, and for a moment I felt that I was outside my body looking down on the city and the field below as the warriors on each side scurried about in their chaotic dance. A shout in the distance brought me back into focus, and I watched a series of large scaling ladders being moved from the rear toward the Saracens' front lines.

Sir Thomas took the chain mail and sword from me as the parapet around us became crowded with men and equipment, and before long, the cries of the army below and those of our own forces had created a fearsome din. With a mighty shout, the Saladin's lines surged forward, the Saracens charging across the ground. At the same time, their archers released a fusillade of thousands of arrows high into the sky, aiming to drop them on top of us. Forcing us to take cover would also let their troops advance unhindered to the base of our walls.

I dropped to my knees, huddling close to the parapet, trying to make myself as small as possible. The arrows whizzed through the air, one striking the ground not three feet from me. I tried hard to ignore the screams and cries as some found their targets.

An order was given to return fire, and from all around, our archers stood and fired at the surge of men rushing toward us from below. I looked up to see another raft of arrows coming at us from the Saladin's rear guard. It became impossible to keep an eye on everything. Down below, the Saracens had nearly reached the base of the wall, although our archers were making them pay with every step they took.

Arrows fell out of the sky, landing all around, and I saw one of the men-at-arms struck down right in front of me. I still had my short sword strapped to my belt, but with shaking hands I grasped the pike, the long iron spear he'd dropped when hit by the arrow. I held it firmly, testing its weight, when I saw the tops of several scaling ladders clear the parapets and realized that the Saracens had arrived.

Sir Thomas stood atop one of the battlements shouting, "Forward! To the ladders!" Our men surged forth, pushing the ladders backward with their pikes, swords and bare hands. A few Saracens had nearly reached the top, and their screams added to the racket as they fell backward into the swirling mass of their comrades below.

I found an open spot along the parapet. The top of an enemy ladder appeared in front of me and I pushed at it with the pike, trying to topple it backward. But I couldn't manage, and to my shock I saw a Saracen appear. I stood frozen in place as he climbed over the ladder, his face sweating with the effort. Coming to my senses, I grasped the pike in both hands, backed up a few steps and charged at him, shouting, "Beauseant!" at the top of my lungs.

He easily parried my thrust with his scimitar, and I nearly lost my grip on the spear. I jabbed at him again, and he pushed the pike aside again, this time stepping sideways and pulling it from my hands. He came rushing at me, and I fumbled at the short sword at my belt, certain that I was about to die.

With a loud scream he raised the sword above his head with both hands, when a look of shock appeared on his face and he crumpled to the ground. There behind him stood Quincy, holding a pike of his own that he had used to dispatch the Saracen. Quincy stared at me a moment, then nodded and ran along the parapet, finding another spot to defend.

It was this man about to kill me who brought me to my senses. It became clear in that moment that even though I was scared beyond reason, I could not let the fear overtake me or I would surely die.

More ladders came at the walls, and those we pushed back were righted and climbed again. For more than an hour that morning, the Saracens tried vainly to breach the walls. Finally, when the Saladin saw he could not get enough men through without taking heavy casualties, the attack ended. We hurried about, tending to our injured and repairing and replacing weapons, for we knew the Saladin would keep coming, never stopping until he found a way to regain the city.

So the siege began. For days, then weeks, we sat inside our fortress, and I was reminded of a turtle huddled inside its shell. They would poke and prod at us and we would snap back, driving them off after a furious battle. Then days would go by with no activity at all. The attacks seemed to happen most often in the morning, after the Saracens had prayed themselves into a fighting frenzy, and then the arrows flew and the siege engines fired and on they came. Yet try as they might, they could not break us.

Weeks became months, with no break in this pattern. One morning, a second large force of Saracens joined the Saladin's army, another five thousand men by Sir Basil's count. So many tents dotted the plains below us that it was nearly impossible to see a bare spot of ground. When this new group arrived, the enemy lines were strangely silent, and about the only time there appeared to be any activity at all was during their daily prayers.

Each day the tension grew. The anticipation kept us all on edge and gnawed at the men inside the walls. Arguments became more frequent, fights broke out, and I heard the mumbles and whispers of men who felt cornered. They often talked of sneaking away before being caught or killed. Such thoughts never entered my mind, for despite the tension, I'd come to believe that somehow we would prevail. Sir Thomas reminded everyone that the Saladin could not sustain this siege forever, not with the Lionheart to the east, by now threatening Jerusalem. We spent hours discussing strategy, and debating whether the King would send aid or push on toward the interior. Some believed the King would return at any moment, but one night, after mass, I overhead Sir Thomas tell Sir Basil that no aid was likely to come. The Lionheart would gladly sacrifice Acre if he could fulfill his dream of returning the Holy City to Christian control.

One evening, as twilight approached, I walked up the stone steps leading to the eastern parapet. I had scarcely found an open spot where I could see the plains below me when the now familiar chanting began, the trumpets sounded, and the Saladin's siege engines and archers filled the sky. This time however, I watched in horrid fascination as a giant siege engine, one of the largest I'd ever seen, was pulled forward through the Saracen lines. It began hurling large boulders at the city gates. Every few minutes, it fired and the walls shook with the force of the impact. Our archers took aim and shot at it repeatedly, but the Saracens had covered the vulnerable parts of the machine with wooden shielding and the arrows could not penetrate it. Even our ballistae aimed directly at it had no effect. Would the Saladin finally force his way into Acre?

On and on it went, as the machine blasted rock after rock at the gates. With each shot the Saracens cheered, and then when it looked as if the engine was impervious to any retaliation we could bring to bear on it, the Saladin's army seemed to rise up as one. And if that weren't bad enough, a group of black-robed men took up their positions all along the plain that ran in front of the main city gate. I had never seen warriors dressed like this.

Sir Thomas stood a few feet away, huddling with a small group of knights.

"Sire, look! A new group of warriors has joined the fight!" He came to my side. I looked at Sir Thomas, and for the first time I saw something I could only call fear flash across his face. It was there only for the briefest of moments, but I saw it, and it unnerved me.

"*Al Hashshashin,*" he muttered, so quietly I almost couldn't hear him.

"Sire?"

"They are called Al Hashshashin. It translates to 'the Assassins.' Some call them fanatics. They are some of the most ferocious warriors you will ever find. If the Saladin has persuaded Al Hashshashin to fight here with him, then he means to take the city or die," Sir Thomas said.

As if they could hear us talking about them, the Assassins began to wail, and the sound of their cries unnerved me. It was the moaning of a demon, high pitched and terrifying, and I felt a wave of fear wash over me. Soon they were joined by the Saracens, who shouted out war cries of their own.

In wave after wave they began charging toward us.

And something told me that this time we would not turn them back so easily.

oulder after boulder came thundering at the gates. The wave of Saracens hit Acre like a hammer on an anvil. They sent their entire force toward every side of the city, and the scaling ladders sprouted up like weeds among the battlements and parapets.

The giant siege engine disoriented everyone, and for the first few minutes of the onslaught there was nothing but confusion and fear within our ranks. Over the roaring noise, I heard Sir Thomas shouting not far from where I stood.

"To the walls! Forward! Fight!" Finally his words were drowned out by the commotion. He swung his sword back and forth like a demon, striking down man after man. I worked my way through the morass of bodies until I reached his side.

"Tristan! Come with me! To the Knights' Hall! Hurry!" he shouted. He turned me toward the steps leading down from the battlements, pushing me forward. I didn't understand at first. Fighting was going on all around us, and Sir Thomas was headed in the other direction.

At the bottom of the steps he took the lead and raced through the streets. The roar of the fighting receded, and the center of the city seemed eerily calm as we ran. In a few moments we burst through the door of our room in the Knights' Hall.

Sir Thomas' tunic was caked in dust and blood. A vicious cut on his left arm still bled. Without a word, I tore a piece of cloth from my own shirt and wrapped it tightly around the wound.

He strode quickly to the table and began writing on a piece of parchment.

"Tristan, we're about to be overrun. There is time for only one last lesson in tactics. What would you, as a soldier, do in this situation?"

I hesitated for a moment, wondering how Sir Thomas could remain so calm amid the chaos that surrounded us. Even though we had been fighting steadily for weeks now, he was, like always, calm, cool and completely in control of his emotions.

"Sire, I'm not sure what you're asking . . . I . . ."

"Quickly, think! You are a Templar; you fight to the last man. Surrender is not an option. So what do you do?"

I tried to change the subject.

"Sire, we must see to your injuries," I said.

"No time for that now," he said. "You can't surrender, you can't escape. What is your plan?"

"I would look for a place to make a last stand," I said.

"Excellent! But where? Here we are, inside a walled city, about to be overrun. Where would you fight? What ground would you choose?"

I thought for a moment.

"The Crusaders' Palace, sire," I said. "The palace is the place I'd pick. It is well built, the thick sandstone walls can withstand fire, and it will cost the Saladin many soldiers to overrun it."

"Well done!" Sir Thomas said. "It would appear that I have trained you well. To the palace we shall go. But tell me, lad. If you had something that could not, must not, fall into enemy hands, how would you attempt escape from this place?"

I thought for a moment. Part of me wanted to just open the door, grab Sir Thomas and find a horse and ride out. We would take our chances trying to make our way through enemy lines rather than be overrun by Saracens, trapped inside the city as we were.

"Quickly. Think!"

"The caves! Most of the Saladin's men are deployed against the city walls. I would try to reach the caves below us, then attempt to sneak past whatever forces hold them, make my way along the shore, and when clear of the enemy lines, climb up the cliff side and follow the coastline until I reached safety."

"Ah, but how would you get to the caves, lad? The city is surrounded. There is no way in or out," he said.

Try as I might, I had no answer. "I don't know, sire," I said. "I'm afraid I don't know." I shrugged, disappointed that I could not come up with an answer.

"Don't worry, Tristan, you've done well. You've done quite well."

Finishing whatever it was he had written, Sir Thomas walked to the fireplace. He grasped a small dagger lying on the mantel and used it to pry a rock loose from the hearth. When the rock was removed, I could see an empty space behind it. Sir Thomas reached into the hole with his good arm and pulled out a leather satchel.

"You have but one last duty for me," he said, hanging the leather satchel on my shoulder.

"We Templars have guarded what you now hold since our earliest days. In time, it has become almost the very reason for our existence. I've told you the story of our founding. We are the Warrior Monks sent by the King of Jerusalem to protect pilgrims traveling on the roads to and from the Holy Land. As our numbers and influence have grown, we've become guardians of many of the relics of our faith: the Ark of the Covenant, the One True Cross and this, the Holy Grail. Christendom's most sacred objects are safeguarded and protected by Templar Knights. And they must be kept safe at all costs. Do you understand?"

"Yes, sire," I said.

I felt my heart sink. Sir Thomas had just handed me the most venerable and mysterious relic in the history of mankind.

I knew the story of the Holy Grail. Or at least some of the stories, I should say. Many did not believe it even existed. Some said the Templars kept the Grail safe. I'd had no idea that it was true.

"Only the Master of the Order and a handful of carefully chosen brothers know the truth and the locations of these relics. The Grail is never kept in one place for long in case someone outside our circle should learn of its whereabouts. We were not able to move it before the Saladin surrounded us. With the city lost, we cannot chance it being found. So I entrust it to you. You must tell no one that you have it, not even another Templar.

"The satchel has a false bottom," he said, taking the bag back. He opened it and showed me how the layer of leather that lay across the bottom of the satchel covered a secret compartment. When he pushed down on the edge of the satchel's bottom, I saw that a small tab of leather popped out of the lining. Pulling up on the tab, he lifted the leather covering, and there, wrapped in several layers of white linen cloth, lay the Grail.

Sir Thomas replaced the false bottom, closed the bag and handed it to me. I placed it on my shoulder, with the strap around my neck. I had no wish to look upon the Grail, no desire to unwrap it from its linen covering and gaze upon its wonders. At that moment I only wished I'd never heard of it. I knew that Sir Thomas was about to order me away from him, and it was an order I had no desire to follow.

"You will carry this satchel to Tyre and find passage to England. You must take what I have given you to Scotland, to the Church of the Holy Redeemer near Rosslyn. Father William is the priest there. He will know what to do. Give it to no one but him. Do you understand? I will stay and hold the palace with the other knights as long as possible. I trust no one but you. And you know that what you carry can never leave your side. If the Saladin were to capture it . . ." Sir Thomas shuddered.

"But, sire!"

"No. It is done." Gathering his strength, Sir Thomas rose to his feet. He fumbled at a small cloth bag hanging from his belt, placing it inside the satchel.

"There are coins in the bag. Enough to get you to England, and a letter from me should you need to explain yourself to anyone," he said.

"Sire, please, if we leave now, we can escape. As you said, there are Templar regimentos in Tyre. I have heard the men-at-arms say that this attack cannot be sustained. The Saladin's forces may take the city, but if we retreat . . ."

"Ah, Tristan. This is the first time I have given you an order and you have questioned it. No. I cannot leave. I will die here defending the palace or we shall prevail and drive the Saladin from this place.

127

But you must go—now. What you carry is the rarest thing left in this world, and men will kill for it without thinking twice. Trust no one. Not even another Templar. I have seen what possession of this thing can do to men. It has turned even my brothers of the Temple into glory-crazed hounds. It must not ever leave your side until you reach Rosslyn. Are we clear?"

I slumped. I couldn't leave him! Since I'd left my home at St. Alban's, he had been like a father to me. How could I take my leave while he stayed behind? I knew what fate awaited him if he remained here.

Sir Thomas walked slowly across the room and laid his sword upon the wooden table. He picked up his helmet, placing it on his head.

"You have been a joy to me, Tristan. Lancelot himself had no more faithful squire," he said.

I knew that nothing I could do or say would sway him. Sir Thomas was not an overly stubborn man, just sworn to duty. And duty came above all else.

He was about to speak again when a call to arms came from the courtyard outside the room. And beyond the shouts and sounds of running feet, we could hear the war cry of the Saladin's soldiers in the streets outside. They had finally breached the walls!

"Come, lad, we must get you to the palace. You were right in your assessment. The way out of Acre is through the caves. In the temple at the palace there is a hidden passage. With luck you can safely make your way to Tyre and find a ship to England. Until you leave Outremer, travel only at night and rest by day. Keep a sharp eye. You should be able to make it there in two weeks, maybe less."

Sir Thomas did not wait for my answer but turned toward the

door as the cries of the warriors in the courtyard grew to a fever pitch. Before I knew what was happening, the door to the room exploded off its hinges and a Saracen burst into the room. He wore a green and white striped turban and looked terrifying. With a vicious yell, a sound so frightening it froze me in place, he raised his gleaming scimitar and came thundering across the room directly at Sir Thomas.

17

I watched in horror as the Saracen's blade whistled through the air toward Sir Thomas' head. My hand went to the hilt of my sword, but before I could move from the spot, Sir Thomas blocked the downward swing of the scimitar, spun on one heel and brought his sword around in a mighty stroke, striking the man down.

"Hurry, boy! Now!" he shouted. He jumped over the body of the man who lay bleeding on the floor, through the door and into the courtyard.

The main compound of the city was chaos. Men yelled and horses wailed, and the sound of the battle was deafening. Looking along the main street leading from our quarters I saw only a mass of men, knights and men-at-arms in chain mail fighting Saracens in turbans. In these last few months of the siege we had seen skirmish after skirmish and attack after attack as the Saracens had tried to overrun our walls. But nothing like this. How could they have finally fought their way inside the city?

The sky rained fire. Flaming arrows descended from the heavens, and the thumping sound of siege engines could be heard flinging clay pots of burning oil onto the rooftops of the city. I could hear the whistle of the quarrels fired from the ballistae, like arrows shot from the bow of a giant, and the screams as they found their targets. The brothers would have said that it looked as if the gates of hell itself had opened before us.

Another knight, his mail coat caked in mud and blood, ran past us on his way toward a small group of approaching Saracens.

"They broke through the west gate," he shouted. "We will rally at the Crusaders' Palace! Hurry!"

Running a few yards in front of us he launched himself at three attackers. Caught off guard by this approach the whole of them tumbled to the ground, wrestling and fighting hand to hand in the mud of the street.

"My back, lad! Keep a sharp eye!" Sir Thomas shouted, starting down the street as quickly as his battered body would carry him. Surprisingly, we ran untouched by the fighting surrounding us until we reached the first cross street of the main thoroughfare. My sword was in my hand, but I had no memory of drawing it.

As we passed through the intersection of the street, Saracens came rushing toward Sir Thomas, but veered in my direction when they saw me behind him, thinking a young boy an easier target than a knight. The smaller of the two raised his weapon, screaming in rage. I managed to block his first downward thrust, but his sword was much heavier, and my blade flew from my hand. He swung at my head with all his might, and I barely managed to duck. His momentum spun him around so that his back was facing me. I jumped forward, throwing my shoulder into him and knocking him to the ground.

"Run, Tristan!" I heard Sir Thomas say as he pulled at my arm.

I glanced around and saw the other attacker lying nearby, apparently dispatched by Sir Thomas while I was otherwise occupied. As I grabbed my dropped sword, he pushed me farther down the street and on we ran.

After several minutes of picking and fighting our way through the chaos we reached our destination.

The Crusaders' Palace was a small city within a city. Like Acre, it was surrounded by walls. Each corner section held a tower that was manned by several knights, archers and men-at-arms.

The Saladin's forces were making their way through the streets methodically, building by building, but they had not yet reached the palace. Ahead of us we saw a small group of Templars outside the palace gate, weapons at the ready.

"Hurry, Tristan, not much time," said Sir Thomas as we sprinted up the steps through the main gate into the courtyard of the palace. None of the Templars paid us any mind as they and their squires rushed back and forth inside and out of the gate, preparing to make a final stand.

Sir Thomas pushed his way through a small crowd gathering inside, and I followed him across the courtyard. Inside the palace was a small temple where the knights held their ceremonies and the priests conducted mass. Small as it was, it was quite beautiful, with thick walls canceling out some of the noise and confusion from outside.

Sir Thomas strode quickly to the altar. It stood waist high and was made of stone. The top surface was a flat section of marble that had been polished to a high sheen. Sir Thomas laid his bloody sword on the altar and reached below the top, pushing on one of the stones making up the altar's base. It popped inward a few inches and with his hip he pushed against the marble top. The altar swiveled on a pivot to reveal a small wooden door in the floor below it. A secret passage! But where did it lead?

Sir Thomas lifted the door, and I could see a ladder leading down into the darkness. He crossed the floor to the sacristy door and removed a torch from its holder on the wall. He tossed the still lighted torch into the hatch, and it hit the ground but kept burning, illuminating a tunnel leading away from the ladder.

"You must go, Tristan," he said. "This tunnel eventually takes you to the caves below the city. They will likely be guarded by only a handful of Saracens. You must make your way past them, travel along the shore until you are safe, then climb up to the main road. Remember, you must travel only at night. Stay in sight of the road so you don't get lost, but do not travel directly on it. You might encounter more of the enemy."

Outside, the sounds of the battle grew nearer. Our enemies were closing in on the palace, and the knights in the courtyard were putting up a ferocious defense. Across the room I saw Quincy and Sir Basil. Sir Basil held a large battle-ax in his left arm while Quincy affixed a large bandage to his right shoulder. When he finished, Sir Basil moved toward the door of the palace, where the fighting outside had grown louder. Quincy followed bravely behind him. Would I ever see them again?

Unbuckling his belt Sir Thomas handed me the sword, scabbard and all, and then pulled his Templar ring off his finger, shoving it inside the satchel.

"These may come in handy. Don't be afraid to use them," he said.

"But sire, you'll need your sword!" I pleaded.

He waved me off. "Don't worry. There are plenty of weapons here," he said.

Choking back tears, I slipped the belt over my shoulders so the sword was at my back, and made sure the satchel was secure.

I looked at Sir Thomas. "Sire . . . please . . . ," I pleaded.

"Tristan, lad . . . there is no time for this. As your knight I have given you an order, and I expect you to obey it. Now go," he said, pushing me toward the hatch.

I stepped onto the ladder, beginning my descent. As I looked up at Sir Thomas for the last time, he reached out to touch me on the shoulder.

"Tristan," he said, his eyes filling with tears. "Beauseant! Beauseant, lad!"

Be glorious.

Tears started then, but I knew nothing would change his mind.

Descending into the darkness of the tunnel, I was convinced I had seen Sir Thomas for the last time. I heard the sound of the altar moving back over the hatch above me, and then noises of the nearby battle faded completely.

Picking up the torch, I quickly made my way through the tunnel. Several yards in, the tunnel became more like a stairway descending into the earth below the city. I did not know how long the torch would burn, so I moved as fast as possible. I didn't like being in such a small, enclosed space. The air was dank and moist, and I found it hard to breathe. Sweat lined my face, and I brushed it from my eyes. Step after step, I continued until I felt the air becoming cooler, and could smell the ocean.

Eventually I found myself inside a large cavern and stopped to listen. In the far distance I heard the sound of water as waves washed up on the shore. Nearby were the quiet murmurs of voices and the sounds of men.

Extinguishing the torch in the dirt floor of the cavern, I waited a few moments for my eyes to adjust to the darkness, but even then it was hard to see. The smell of the ocean was stronger now, and after a moment I saw a faint flicker of light ahead, whether from torches or a fire I could not tell.

Keeping to the wall of the cavern, I left the tunnel opening and slowly and quietly made my way toward the light. The first cavern gave way to a larger one, and I crept softly forward. A dim light began to cut the darkness.

Sir Thomas had been right. Saracens were in the cavern ahead of me. The noise of the ocean grew louder, and I realized they must be sitting just inside the cave opening on the beach. It was only by luck that they had not yet discovered the passage at the rear.

Cautiously, I peered around the corner of the cavern. About twenty paces ahead of me sat three of the Saladin's warriors huddled around a fire. Each of them had a tremendously long scimitar at his belt, and one of them held a giant and deadly looking battle-ax.

The sound of the waves had dimmed the noise of the battle in the city above, but now and then I heard shouts and explosions. I ducked back around the corner of the cavern, needing to think of a plan, a diversion that would get me past these men and onto the beach. I fingered the satchel that hung on my shoulder and offered up a silent prayer, hoping for some sign or guidance to get me out of this predicament. A miracle would also be welcome. A small miracle would be fine. Nothing too serious. No lightning strikes necessary. Just . . .

At that moment, I heard the sound of a trumpet, and the men in the cave jumped to their feet, talking rapidly in Arabic. The horn must have sounded a call to arms, and from what I could guess, the soldiers were arguing over whether or not to abandon their posts or hold their positions in the cave. Two pointed up toward the battle above, while the third shook his head, pointing at the ground where he stood, muttering something. I assume he meant to stay rooted to his spot.

At last they came to some agreement. Two of the men ran out of the cave, disappearing from sight. The remaining guard sat back down at the fire, unfortunately still facing me with the giant scimitar. Very long and sharp this scimitar was. At least the size of a small tree, I was certain.

I needed to escape before his companions returned, but how could I defeat a trained warrior of the Saladin in hand-to-hand combat? I needed something to give me some advantage. Finally an idea came to me.

Reaching down I grabbed a handful of sand. I quietly drew my short sword and peered around the corner of the cavern to make sure the soldier remained in the same spot. I took a deep breath, gathered my will and jumped out of the cavern, screaming a war cry at the top of my lungs.

The man yelled in surprise, but being well trained, he recovered quickly and jumped to his feet. I ran a few paces directly at him, watching in horror as he drew the scimitar, certain that it measured at least eleven feet long. I hoped my plan would work.

By the time I was a few feet away, his arm had drawn back the scimitar, which would likely remove my head as he brought it around. At the peak of his backswing, I threw the handful of sand in his face.

Temporarily blinded he shrieked, clutching at his eyes with his free hand and trying to see. Staggering backward he began swinging the giant sword all about, blind with rage. I danced away from him, still yelling to cover the sounds of my movement.

In a second I was behind him. I brought the hilt of my sword down on his head as hard as I could. He cried out, falling to the ground, and went silent.

Quickly moving to the campfire I kicked sand on it until the flames went out. I didn't want anyone passing the cave to spot me in the firelight. The man on the ground behind me groaned. There was no time to waste.

I saw Saracens moving about here and there on the beach, luckily too far away to have heard their comrade's cry. Moving from the safety of the cave I crept as quickly as I could along the cliff face, darting from boulder to boulder, finding whatever cover there was. It took me more than an hour to move even a half league. Several times I dove behind a pile of rocks as soldiers rushed by, but as the darkness of the night deepened, eventually I managed to put the cave and the city of Acre above it behind me.

When I had seen or heard no one for half an hour or so, I began looking for a place where I could scale the cliffs and reach the road to Tyre. A few leagues from the cave I found a trail leading from the rocks along the shore up the side of the cliffs.

The path was steep and narrow, cutting back and forth along the rock face. It was a hard climb, and soon I was sweating, my breath coming in shallow gasps. I stopped to rest several times, always hugging the cliff, praying that I would meet no one coming down from the top. It would be a simple matter to be pushed or thrown from the narrow trail, and that meant sure death on the rocks below.

After another hour of climbing, I reached the cliff top. I paused momentarily to catch my breath, then cautiously made my way inland from the cliffs toward the road.

Cresting a small rise, I looked back toward Acre. The city was in flames. Even from that distance the wind still carried the sounds of battle—the screams and shouts of dying men and above it all, a high-pitched, eerie wail that will forever haunt my sleep. The sound that told me all was lost.

The cry of Al Hashshashin.

On the Road to Tyre

18

I t was near dawn on the third night after my escape from Acre. Following Sir Thomas' instructions, I rested during the day, finding a group of rocks or some wooded glen to sleep in, and traveled near but never directly on the main road to Tyre. I was able to fill my water skin in the many streams and springs on this part of the coast. The wild olive, fig and date trees that dotted the countryside provided me with food.

From the shadows, I watched many groups of men pass by me in the darkness. A large detachment had ridden by the previous night, but with the cloudy sky, I could not tell if they were friend or foe. It was better to remain alone than risk capture and sure death at the hands of the Saladin's forces.

Before I fell asleep each morning, I worried over the Grail. I knew that Sir Thomas saw its safety as my duty, but it weighed me down as if I'd been tossed into the sea with a millstone about my neck. I reminded myself that Sir Thomas, the man I admired and respected like no other, had chosen *me* for this sacred duty. I should have been honored.

Part of me was angry with Sir Thomas. "Here, Tristan, take the

Grail back to England. Don't let anyone near it, Tristan. Keep it safe at all times, Tristan." Horse dung. I wished I'd had the courage to stand up to Sir Thomas. That I had demanded to stay in Acre, as my duty commanded.

Then I realized that I was alive, that I owed Sir Thomas my life. And I was grateful.

The night was nearly over. Soon I would need to find a safe place to sleep for the day. I found it hard to concentrate. There was danger all about me, yet the fate of Sir Thomas and the other knights was all I thought of. I missed Quincy and Sir Basil and tried to force myself not to think of what I knew their fate must have been. I told myself that somehow, the knights at the palace had managed to turn back the Saracens. I held that thought, small comfort that it was.

Perhaps because I was not paying attention, the bandits surrounded me before I realized my mistake.

"Hold!" a voice said out of the darkness.

My hand moved toward the short sword at my belt. Sir Thomas' battle sword was still strapped to my back, but was too difficult to draw without notice.

"Don't do it," the voice said again. From the accent, I could tell it was an Englishman. And for a moment I felt the relief wash through me that I had not stumbled upon a group of Hashshashin. But then I remembered: bandits. Bands of these men, who had grown weary of the Crusade, roamed the countryside, preying on the weak and defenseless while they made their way homeward. Englishmen and Christians they were, and most likely deserters.

"My name is Tristan St. Alban," I said. "Servante of Sir Thomas Leux of the Knights Templar. Who commands me to hold?"

There was no response. Only silence. The night was cloudy, and I could only make out a dim shape several paces in front of me. Off to my right and left I sensed movement but saw nothing. All of them were well out of reach of my sword.

Finally the voice. "State your business," it commanded.

"I am gathering forage for the horses. Our camp is yonder." I needed to convince them, whoever they were, that I was not alone.

Again, silence. There were a few hushed whispers among them, but I could not determine what was being said.

"I think not, boy," the voice said. "I think you are alone. There is no camp about. We would have seen it. Now, very slowly, draw your sword and lower it to the ground."

There was no further sound for a moment. I heard the barest whisper of movement as those on my right and left moved to take a position behind me. They would surround and try to rush me, so I kept my hand on the hilt of my sword.

"You would assault a servante of the Templars?" I asked. "Are you mad? They will hunt you down, and you will know no mercy if you harm one of their own."

"If you serve the Templars, as you say," the voice replied, "we will be long gone before you are able to rejoin them. Now, this can end quickly and easily or with difficulty. Lower your sword and hand over that satchel and bedroll."

His words told me they had been following me for some time, and if so, they definitely knew I was alone.

The moon was setting low in the sky but broke through the clouds and began giving shadows to the darkness of the woods. Ahead of me perhaps ten paces, the dim outline of a man grew less faint. He held a worn sword in his left hand and was dressed in shabby clothing. I could not make out much else, except that he was bearded and wore a cloth hat pulled low and close to his eyes.

Looking quickly to my right and left I could not yet see either of the other men. Sure that they had moved behind me, I tightened my hand on my sword, and with the other I firmly gripped the satchel. I was about to take flight when two sets of arms grabbed me roughly from behind.

"Let me go! Let me go!" I shouted. "Sir Thomas! Sir Basil! Help! Bandits!"

Of course, there were no knights nearby, but I hoped to confuse and delay the thieves all the same. Holding fiercely to the satchel, I managed to free my other arm momentarily, scratching and clawing and punching at the arms holding me. The man to the front of me started toward me with his sword raised.

I kicked and hollered and screamed mightily, but was outnumbered and considerably outmuscled. I started gasping for breath, for each time I yelled, the arms holding me grew tighter around my chest.

Then a very strange thing happened. The man who held me yelled loudly in my ear, followed by another painful scream a second later. His arms let loose and he staggered forward, falling to the ground. To my great surprise I saw in the dim light that two arrows had magically appeared in his backside and a large red stain darkened his pants, moving outward from each arrow's shaft. He shrieked, wiggling on the ground, clutching at his buttocks.

From behind me a loud voice commanded, "Drop your weapons!"

The man in front of me paused, unsure what to do. The other man to the side of me released his grip on the satchel, and as he did so, I drew my short sword and jumped sideways away from him. He and his companion were confused, not knowing where the voice had come from, but realizing the situation had turned.

"Now! Drop your swords or my next arrow finds a throat and not an arse!" the voice shouted. "I have a wallet full of arrows and haven't shot a bandit in a week, so move one more step toward the lad and see what sport a King's Archer can make with swine like you!"

A King's Archer? Here in the woods?

The bandits were silent. Their wounded companion struggled to his feet and had clearly lost his taste for thievery. He staggered past the leader of the group, howling like a wounded pig. In moments he had disappeared into the woods.

I kept my sword up and pointed toward the bandit closest to me.

"Very well," the archer shouted from the woods behind us. "My arm grows weary. Perhaps I'll just shoot you both and be done with it! The world could use two fewer bandits!"

It was not to be, however. The bandit closest to me ran, and I pivoted to face the leader. As I did so, I drew Sir Thomas' battle sword from behind me, holding it in my right hand with the short sword in my left.

"Time to run," I said.

As the bandit's face grew more distinct in the gathering light, I could see a look of anger clouding his features. He had failed to rob an easy mark, and it did not sit well.

"I will see you again, squire of the Templars," he muttered. But as he started to turn, an arrow whistled past my ear, taking the bandit's hat off his head. I nearly laughed as I watched it land with a solid thud in the trunk of a tree ten paces beyond him. The bandit froze.

"If *I* see *you*," the voice shouted, "the last thing *you* will see is my arrow, seconds after it pierces your chest, so I hope you'll please me by making more idle threats. The King requires me to kill ten bandits a month, and so far I'm one short."

But the bandit didn't hear the last part. Losing his hat had clearly unnerved him. He disappeared into the woods before the last words of the archer had echoed off the trees.

My shoulders slumped and I felt myself go limp. I was angry with myself for walking so blindly into a trap, yet relieved at being alive. Remembering the archer with the itchy temperament behind me I sheathed both swords and looked in the direction of the voice, my hands empty and held out from my sides.

"Hello? Archer?" I said to the woods behind me. I still saw no one. "I thank you for your help!" I did not speak too loudly for who knew what other dangers these woods held? If there were three bandits nearby, there were likely thirty.

"Hello?" I said again. "Will you not come forward, so that I may thank you face-to-face?"

Then I saw him. From twenty paces away he stepped from behind a wild olive tree and walked to where I stood. He was taller than I but wore the colors of the King, and in his left hand he carried the traditional longbow made of yew. On his back sat a wallet full of arrows, the gray feathers riding above his head. He was thick through the arms and chest like most archers I had seen. His hair and face were fair in color. Close up I could see his features clearly, and was startled to see that he was young—my age, or perhaps a year or two older.

I extended my hand. "I owe you both thanks and my life," I said. He cautiously looked at me, then took my hand, shaking it briefly. "My name is Tristan."

"Robard," he answered. "My name is Robard Hode, formerly of the King's Archers."

"If I may inquire, what brings you to these woods?" I asked.

"My conscription is over. I'm on my way back to England," he replied.

And that is how I first met Robard Hode, born in Sherwood Forest near the shire of Nottingham.

obard had traveled here from the south near Jerusalem. He did not know of the fall of Acre, which had been his destination. I told him that Acre was in the Saladin's hands, and he agreed we could travel to Tyre together. When he asked me why I chose to travel at night, I explained to him that I carried dispatches for the Templars there, and dared not allow these documents to fall into the hands of the enemy. He accepted my explanation without much question.

I was grateful to have Robard and his bow as traveling companions. As before, we kept to the hills near the main road. At night we built no fires. Walking in the darkness we quietly exchanged the stories of our lives.

Robard was seventeen years old. His father owned a large farm near the shire of Nottingham. When King Richard took the throne and raised his army for the Crusades, he levied taxes on all the farmers of England. After a poor harvest two years before, Robard's father had been unable to meet his burden. Those who could not pay were allowed to join the army or send a son in their stead to join the Crusaders. Robard joined the King's Army, and after two years of service, his father's debt was forgiven.

It was Robard's father who first taught him to use the bow. And two years of nearly constant warfare had made him an exceptional archer. In the King's Army he learned that an archer was only as good as his equipment. Before we slept each morning, Robard obsessively checked his bow for signs of wear or weakness. He studied and re-checked the hide strings that held the grip, a piece of wood fastened to the shaft. He removed every arrow from his wallet, checking the feathers and the points to make sure they were secure and sharp. Each morning, when it was light enough to see clearly, he would take several practice shots at a distant tree. Retrieving the arrows from the trunk, he checked them again, returning them to his wallet.

As we traveled, Robard told me much of his life and what he had witnessed during his years in Outremer.

"I've seen nothing but waste and destruction," he complained. "The Lionheart"—Robard spat out the name as if something sour and unpleasant had landed on his tongue—"commands us to take a fortress or a city or a swatch of land, and we do. Then a few weeks or months later the Saladin's forces take it back. Men are killed for nothing. Yet the King keeps raising his army and taking more taxes while poor men like my father struggle to feed their families."

Robard was quietly intense, and when he spoke of his home and father and the struggles of the people of his shire, he became quite passionate. I sensed a great determination in him.

"What will you do when you return to England?" I asked when he finally paused in his rant against King Richard, the rich and the general inequalities of the known world.

"Go home, help my father farm. He'll need it if this war goes on much longer. The rich barons easily pay their taxes to the King while poor folk go hungry, sending their sons to die here in this desert wasteland because they cannot pay."

Robard was a bitter young man on the subject of the rich in general, the poor in particular and taxes especially. Though I was certainly no saint, I winced at his reference to the Holy Land as a "wasteland" and quietly crossed myself.

"I knew a man at home," Robard went on, "a farmer, like my father, with seven children. After the poor harvest two years ago there wasn't much in the way of food for such a large family. One day he went off into Sherwood Forest and killed a roebuck. On his way home he stumbled across a squad of bailiffs led by the shire reeve of Nottingham. As usual, the shire reeve and his men were out collecting taxes from poor farmers who couldn't afford to pay them even if gold were to grow out of the ground like beans. They saw him with the buck and attempted to arrest him, saying he had no authority to hunt the King's deer."

Robard's voice rose. I wished to quiet him, lest more bandits or, God forbid, the Saladin's men heard us in the woods.

"But before they could grab him he escaped into the woods. As far as I know, he's still there hiding out. All because he wanted enough meat to feed his children," he said. "That is who I am forced to fight for. We serve an absent King who cares nothing for his subjects, only that they can send their sons to feed his army. He leaves his sniveling coward of a brother Prince John in charge, and that poor excuse for a monarch allows the shire reeves to rule the countryside like barons. Lionheart, my arse," Robard said, spitting on the ground for emphasis.

"What of the man and his family?" I asked.

"Ha!" Robard said. "When they couldn't catch him, the shire reeve arrested his wife instead, confiscated his lands and sent his children off to orphanages. When I return, I hope that fat shire reeve makes a move toward arresting me for something." Robard held his bow out in front of him, and pantomimed shooting an arrow.

I thought perhaps it might be best to change the subject, so I told Robard some of my history, my time with the monks and how I came to be the squire of a Templar Knight.

"Raised by monks, you say?" he asked.

"Yes."

"Then you can read and write?"

"Of course," I said almost incredulously. Then I cringed, realizing Robard had asked me this because he could not. I had taken it for granted. The monks who raised me were learned men who saw to it that I was educated. The Templars were also men of letters. Robard had been born a peasant. No one had ever taught him. He looked at me intently for a moment, then glanced away. I wondered if this had changed his opinion of me. Hoping I hadn't embarrassed him, I quickly changed the subject, telling him of my service with Sir Thomas.

After that, Robard seldom asked questions about my life and I did not offer more than the barest of details. Still, I was glad to have him along. He was well trained and had showed courage in facing down the bandits. So far I had enjoyed his company—as long as I kept the conversation away from taxes, King Richard, shire reeves, the Holy Land, noblemen, the Saladin and the rich.

We made much better time traveling together. I had no doubt

there were others in the woods and on the road who spotted us at some point. But together we were more formidable. We kept moving ever eastward toward Tyre.

On the early morning of our third day together, Robard shot a hare. Deep in the woods we built a fire with very dry wood that gave off little smoke. We roasted the hare and ate a fine meal, the first meat I had eaten since leaving Acre.

We made many miles at night and in the predawn hours bedded down in a rocky outcropping a few hundred yards off the main road. Tall boulders surrounded us on three sides, making a U-shaped enclosure, with the open side to the west, so we would be shaded from the hottest sun while sleeping through the day. Unrolling our blankets on the ground, we were asleep in minutes.

Hours later, a faint and subtle humming sound roused me from sleep, and I was instantly awake. It was still twilight, not quite dark, but I sensed something amiss. I listened. All was quiet. Then a noise, a whisper of movement, came from the woods beyond the boulders.

I rolled quietly to my knees, picking up my short sword. Robard lay a few feet away, snoring softly. Through the opening in the rocks, I could see several yards into the woods, and for a moment, I thought I saw a black-clad figure moving through the trees. Not sure if my eyes were playing tricks, I quietly crawled to Robard, placing my hand over his mouth. He awakened instantly, grabbing at my wrist, but I hissed him to silence, pointing to the opening in the rocks.

"Trouble," I whispered.

He was on his feet in an instant, his bow strung, an arrow nocked and at the ready. Quietly we stepped to the opening in the rocks, taking a position on either side. I left the battle sword on the ground, as it was too long if I needed to fight in such a small enclosed area.

Robard listened, studying the woods. The twilight shadows grew longer and the darkness deepened. I saw nothing, but the woods had gone too quiet. Something was out there. We stood motionless for what felt like hours, but in reality was only a few minutes. I was tense, but Robard appeared calm, holding his bow almost gently in front of him, ready to shoot as soon as he spotted a target.

Then, very clearly we heard movement—a quick rustle of feet through the grass and leaves—but still we saw nothing. Instinct commanded that I look behind me. I glanced to the rocks above our campsite, and there stood a figure clad in a black robe, his face obscured by a black turban and veil.

"Robard!" I shouted. Robard spun, raising his bow as the figure leapt from the rocks above. Then we heard it—that awful, wailing cry. They were upon us.

Al Hashshashin.

The Assassins.

20

he wail of the Assassins was deafening. How they had found us, I had no idea, hidden as we were from casual passersby. There was one to our rear, leaping at us through the air, and I was sure there were at least two more in the woods beyond our camp. But their cries were so loud it sounded as if there must be hundreds of them. For a brief moment I wondered how so few men could make such a thunderous racket. It was a horrible high-pitched keening wail that I was sure must be the song of the devil himself.

Robard's arrow took the Assassin high in the shoulder, spinning him around. He landed a few feet away on his back with a resounding thud. The twin daggers he held in each hand bounced on the ground, spinning away from his body.

Almost before I could see it, Robard pulled another arrow from his wallet, and it was nocked and ready as he turned to the front of our encampment, facing the break in the boulders. I could still hear the wailing noise, but it seemed to be coming from nowhere and everywhere at the same time.

"Tristan!" Robard shouted. "We need to move. We're too vulnerable and trapped. Head for that opening yonder." He pointed with the arrow on his bow toward a small clearing in the woods, perhaps thirty yards from where we stood.

I had seen my share of battle with Sir Thomas and the knights, and I knew that Robard had as well. But it seemed foolish to me to leave the safety of the rocks. Then from behind us I heard a clawing sound, clearly another Assassin climbing the boulders to come at us again. At that moment, Robard's plan seemed the best of several bad options.

"You take a running start and tuck and roll out of the opening. I'll follow behind with the bow. I expect there will be at least two of them on either side, thinking they'll capture us as we run out. We'll need to surprise them. You go first and take the one to the right. I'll come behind you and take the one on the left."

"Me first?" I said. "Why not you first?"

I found several parts of Robard's plan to be lacking, starting with the part where I rolled out of the boulders first.

"Tristan!" he shouted again. "I'll cover you!"

"Okay, ready!" I yelled back. Obviously it was a lie, as I was most certainly not ready!

I wanted to take a moment to think of a different plan. But the wailing grew louder, more insistent, and I had no better suggestion. I backed up toward the rear wall of the rocks, keeping an eye over my shoulder, lest the Assassin behind us show himself. Reaching down I slung the satchel over my neck and shoulder.

With a running start, the short sword firmly in my hand, I sprinted toward the opening of the boulders. Just before I cleared the gap, I dropped to the ground and rolled through. I did not see, but heard, and swore I could feel, the whooshing sound of a scimitar swooping through the air where my head had been only an instant before. I heard the clang of steel on rock as I came to my feet, spinning to face my attacker.

It happened almost exactly as Robard had predicted. Two robed Assassins stood on either side of the opening. In an instant they both leapt at me, scimitars raised, and I ducked underneath their wild swings. I heard and felt something go whizzing past my ear. Then an arrow appeared in the back of one of the Assassins. Robard had found his mark quickly.

The remaining Assassin came at me with his sword moving in a vicious downward arc. I blocked the first swing, but as before in the streets of Acre, a scimitar is a much heavier weapon than the small sword I held, and the force of the Assassin's blow sent it spinning from my hand. Now I was defenseless, for I had left Sir Thomas' battle sword inside the ring of boulders.

The Assassin's momentum toppled him into me, and I grabbed at his arms, grappling with him, too late realizing I was between Robard and the attacker. He would not have a clear shot.

The Assassin broke free of my grip. Jumping backward, he screamed in fury, raising his scimitar again and lunging at me. I darted backward. His eyes, all that I could see of his face through his turban and veil, went wild with anger. I was momentarily frozen in fear.

Behind me I heard Robard yell, "Tristan, move! I can't get a clear shot!" But there was nowhere for me to go. The Assassin was lunging again, driving me back between the rocks. I spotted my sword a few feet away. Too far. I wanted to remind Robard that I had been against this plan from the very beginning. However, I doubted the Assassin would allow me any time to rebuke my friend.

The Assassin swung his scimitar at me with two hands. I dodged this first swing while looking wildly about for a rock, a tree branch, anything I could use as a weapon. Then remembering the satchel, I pulled it off my neck and shoulder, wrapping the strap tightly in my right wrist.

"Robard! The battle sword!" I screamed. I could not see Robard, but heard him shouting behind me. I had no idea what he was saying. Probably something about how I had ruined his perfectly good plan by trying to wrestle with an enraged Hashshashin.

I had only one advantage: although the scimitar is a fine weapon, it is heavy and not made for quick thrusts and jabs. It is wielded like a club, crashing down on its victim to break bone and steel or puncture armor. When the Assassin stepped in and swung the sword again in a long looping arc, I moved back and away from the sword tip. As it went by and the attacker's momentum carried him with it, I stepped in and swung the satchel with all my might. I hoped that it wouldn't break my precious cargo, but it was well padded and at the bottom of the satchel. And right now I needed its heft.

It swung out from my wrist like a mace, and I watched it connect solidly with the head of the Assassin. I heard a sound like a melon dropped on a stone floor, and the attacker crumpled to the ground.

"Go!" shouted Robard. He tossed me the battle sword and I caught it by the hilt. I turned and ran, throwing the satchel over my shoulder and scooping up the short sword as I passed by. We sprinted to the clearing and stood back-to-back, making a slow circle, watching the woods for any sign of more Assassins.

We knew that at least four attackers had set upon us. Robard had shot two and I had managed to knock one unconscious. The woods went quiet. The keening wail of the Assassins had stopped as instantly as it had started. The night grew darker, and it was getting harder to see.

A black-clad figure plunged through the opening in the rocks. No arrow protruded from him, so it must have been the one I had heard climbing from the rear. I yelled and Robard turned, letting loose a shot, but the Assassin darted to the side as Robard's arrow struck the rocks behind him. Reaching to the ground he pulled his now-conscious companion to his feet. They dashed into the forest away from the rocks, zigzagging from tree to tree, making it difficult for Robard to shoot. In moments they had vanished.

Robard and I kept quiet, slowly circling in the hushed clearing, waiting for another attack. Silence. For several seconds there was very little sound. Then the noises of the night began to return. The chirp of insects. The call of birds.

"I think they are gone," I said.

Robard still held his bow at the ready. He was tense, arm held in front of him, the muscles coiled. "I don't understand," he said. "Al Hashshashin do not run. They fight to the death."

"Yes. Strange," I agreed.

We circled again, but there was nothing more to see or hear.

"We need to leave," Robard said.

"Agreed."

Robard lowered but did not completely relax his bow, and we cautiously made our way back to the boulders. I held a sword in each hand and we kept a sharp eye, but the woods around us felt empty.

We quickly gathered up our blankets. Our plan was to move as far away from there as quickly as possible. I rolled our blankets together, slinging them over my shoulder. I would carry Robard's blanket tonight, giving him quicker access to his bow and wallet.

We had turned toward the freedom of the woods when I heard a small gasping sound coming from the Assassin who lay on the ground inside the circle of boulders. Robard's arrow had hit him high up in the right shoulder, and as I looked, I could see him moving. Not to attack, but not dead yet either.

"Wait," I said. "He's not dead."

Robard stopped and I approached the Assassin, kicking the daggers out of reach. Another groan, and then his eyes flew open; two black ovals stared up at me in both alarm and hate.

"Careful, he may still be armed," Robard said.

I looked at the wound where the arrow had entered his shoulder. I didn't see much blood, but he wore a black robe and it was hard to tell. When I touched the shaft of the arrow, the Assassin cried out in pain and his eyes shut.

"What do we do now?" I asked, not looking at Robard as I spoke. "He's not dead. If we leave, and if he lives, he may be able to find his companions. We don't need them following us."

Robard had remained quiet while I checked the Assassin's wounds. And as I turned to look at him, awaiting his answer, the blood drained from my face.

"There's only one thing to do," he said.

I felt as if I were falling into quicksand. With my back turned, Robard had pulled an arrow from his wallet, nocked it on his bowstring and pulled it taut. It was now pointed directly at the heart of the wounded Assassin. I struggled to stand, but it felt as if my legs weren't working properly.

Robard drew the bowstring to his cheek, and I could see his fingers twitch as they were about to let it go.

"Robard! No!" I shouted, launching myself toward him. To my horror I saw his fingers release the arrow, and I could only gasp as it flew through the air headed directly for my chest.

21

ime stood still. I felt I could see and hear everything that happened in exact detail. I had leapt from my crouch and thrown myself in front of the helpless Assassin. I watched Robard's fingers twitch as they released the arrow. It left the bow, and in this state of heightened sensation, I heard the twang of the string and saw the shaft move slowly past the sight rest. I could hear Robard's sharp intake of breath and the word *NO!* leave his mouth in a stunned gasp. But it was too late.

The arrow moved with frightening speed. Robard stood but a few paces away. He had no chance of missing at this distance. I thought of many things in the instant before I died. I remembered Sir Thomas, the brothers and even Sir Hugh and his hatred of me. I thought of the musky smell of the stable at the abbey and the quiet shuffle of the monks' sandals as they filed into the chapel for prayer. I heard the sound of the songbirds that called to me each day when I worked in the abbey garden.

I also thought this was a silly way to die—in defense of a man who would undoubtedly have slain me if the situation were reversed. I remembered Sir Thomas, and how he had tried to teach me honor and humility and his lessons that a warrior is humble and compassionate in victory. Then, not quite dead yet, I hoped he would be proud.

I closed my eyes. I heard it pierce my flesh before I felt it. I fell spinning in the air and landed upon my back, feeling the air rush out of my lungs. My eyes opened briefly to see the arrow sticking straight up, and I waited for the flash of burning pain that would be the last thing I experienced on this earth.

Except the pain didn't come.

Robard rushed to my side, dropping to his knees. "My God! Tristan, please, please forgive me! I had no . . . I never thought . . . Please. I did not mean . . ." His eyes were wild and full of fear. He looked at the arrow, protruding as it did from my chest, and tears fell down his cheeks.

I sat up.

Robard gasped. "How? What?" He stared at me in wonderment.

I looked down at my chest and saw a miracle. Strong words, I know, and the brothers would take me to task for assigning such heavenly status to my own mere survival. But to me, it was a miracle, for I knew I should be dead, or at least gravely injured, and I was neither.

Then I saw the source of my miracle and almost wished I were dead instead. There could be only one explanation.

As I had leapt toward Robard from where I crouched beside the Assassin, the satchel that hung around my shoulder had swung upward with my forward momentum. As it did, it had moved to a spot in front of my chest, and Robard's arrow had found not flesh, but the tough leather of the case. I was glad to be alive, but that feeling changed as soon as I noticed that the arrow had punctured the satchel where the Grail lay hidden in the false bottom.

When Robard realized I was alive and unharmed, he began to laugh hysterically, pounding me on the shoulders.

"Oh dear God," he said. Nervous at the thought of what he had nearly done, his questions came rapidly. "Are you all right? Lucky for you that satchel stayed my arrow. Why did you do that? What were you thinking? Are you sure you are not hurt?"

"I'm fine, really. No harm." In truth, I felt sick and wished very much to crawl into the bushes and empty my stomach of my last meal. But I sat there trying to steady my breathing and quiet the rushing sound in my ears.

"Then, Tristan, why? What were you thinking?" he asked.

I faced Robard, seeing a look of genuine curiosity on his face mixed with concern and anguish at what he had nearly done.

"Templars do not kill a defenseless enemy. Such an act is forbidden by our laws. I realize you are not bound by them, but I can't allow you to harm the Assassin while he is injured. It isn't right."

Robard said nothing. He looked away for a moment, then stood and paced a few steps away. "I don't believe in 'rules of warfare,'" he said. "Nothing but foolishness. There are no rules except kill or be killed. Do you forget that he came to murder us in our sleep? To slit our throats while we lay dreaming?"

I finally felt steady enough to rise to my feet. "I don't forget that at all, Robard. And in battle, I would strike him down and not think twice. As to murder, well, you have a point. But they did not murder us. We fought them hand to hand. Therefore, once the fight is over and he is helpless, then his life belongs to us. There is no honor in killing a defenseless man."

"Honor! You sound like the Lionheart," he said. And as always whenever he mentioned the King, he spat in the dirt for emphasis.

I did not know what to do. We really had no time for this. "We can discuss this later. But now we should see to this man's wounds, then be on our way. Before the Assassins return."

Robard paced back and forth several times within the circle of the rocks. Throwing up his hands he stalked off to the opening of the boulders to check over his bow and wallet.

I could not be angry with Robard. In many ways he was right. Anyway, I was glad to have a moment to myself. As much as I did not want to, I needed to look inside the hidden compartment of the satchel. I feared the worst. Robard's arrow might have shattered the most sacred relic in all of Christendom. But to check on it I needed Robard to be gone temporarily. I couldn't risk him seeing what I carried and asking questions.

I knelt by the Assassin. Apparently he had passed out again, but it appeared the bleeding had slowed. The arrow needed to be removed and that would not be pleasant. From what I could see of his face, the Assassin looked young, perhaps my age or even younger. That might have explained why our attackers broke and ran. Perhaps they were initiates and not full-fledged members of the cult. It could also explain why the two of us could drive them off. Otherwise we'd most certainly be dead.

"Robard, a favor if you please? I'm going to need to remove this arrow. Would you mind filling the water skin at the spring we used yonder? And if you could, find a small piece of wood, maybe the size of a finger in diameter. He's going to need something to bite on when I pull it out."

Robard glared at me with disdain, spitting on the ground and looking ready to launch into another round of arguments, but to my relief he took the water skin and left the boulders. He would be gone a few moments at least.

As I removed the satchel from my shoulder, it felt much heavier than I remembered. My nerves were so jangled, it felt for a moment as if I could barely lift it. I pulled the arrow free of the coarse leather and, setting it on the ground, undid the leather tie holding it closed to look inside.

Dumping all of my personal items from the bag, I thought to myself how I would explain this to Father William if I ever reached Rosslyn. "Hello, Father. Sir Thomas Leux sent me with the Grail. So sorry for the damage. Here it is. Well, good-bye then." "The broken Grail, Father? Well now, there's a tale. You see, my friend shot at me with an arrow, and rather than let it pierce my chest, I thought it wise instead to hide behind the cup of the Savior." I would need to come up with a better story.

Lifting up the hidden bottom of the satchel, I held my breath. Robard's arrow had pierced the leather and driven into the linen wrap. This was bad. This was horribly, horribly bad.

I was more nervous than I'd ever been. Here I was, a simple squire, about to lay eyes on something that had been the object of obsession for more than a thousand years. What would it look like? Would it change me? Taking a deep breath I grasped the cloth covering it.

It was a simple chalice made of fired clay, unremarkable, really, for all that had been written and told and made of it. I held history in my hands. Had this cup once held the blood of our Savior?

Was this what men had fought and died over? An arrow shot from a longbow with enough force can easily pierce armor and mail. By all rights, Robard's arrow should have turned it into holy shards. Instead, I found the Grail as it had been placed there by Sir Thomas. No scratches or cracks or defects of any kind.

The Holy Grail had not a mark on it.

olding the Grail in my hands, I could scarcely believe my luck. Pulling it close to my eyes, I turned it slowly, but could find no imperfection of any kind. No scratch or indentation at all. I went limp with relief and quickly rewrapped the Grail in the linen cloth, restoring it to the secret compartment within the satchel. With my fingers, I pushed back on the leather around the space where the arrow had pierced the satchel and found that the hole closed up well and was not very noticeable. At the very least the white cloth would not show through the satchel wall and would hide the Grail well enough until I could find some way to repair the hole.

Pulling the satchel back over my shoulder, I turned my attention to the wounded Assassin on the ground. With my knife I carefully cut into the cloth of his garment around where the arrow had punctured his shoulder. The bleeding had stopped, but the arrow was buried deep in the flesh.

I had seen how Templar physicians removed arrows when injured knights returned from the battlefield. However, I had never *performed* this technique before on any living person. The most efficient way was to push the arrow all the way through, then cut off the arrow-head and pull the shaft back out. This was often not as easy as it sounded, for the arrowhead can encounter bone and muscle, causing more damage. But it was usually better than the damage caused by pulling the arrowhead out the way it went in.

Then there was the pain involved. And the shouts of agony.

I knew, though, that the arrow must come out. To leave it there was not an option. Blood poisoning would set in and then . . . well. There was only certain death after that.

I pulled away the cloth around the shaft of the arrow and examined the wound. As the Assassin had leapt through the air, Robard had indeed made a very good shot. A few inches to the right and the arrow would have missed entirely, but the shaft had found the Assassin's shoulder up high and close to the arm. This was good news, as it meant I might be able to push the arrow through the soft tissue without hitting bone or the shoulder blade. At least in theory.

A few minutes later, Robard returned with the full water skin and the small, sturdy stick I had asked for. He handed them to me without comment. Removing the stopper from the skin I poured fresh water over the wound. The Assassin did not stir.

I couldn't hold up the Assassin and push the arrow through at the same time. I needed Robard's assistance.

"Robard, could you help me here, please?" I asked.

Robard stood to the side of the boulders, scanning the forest. He looked at me and his eyes narrowed.

"Robard, I beg you. I'm aware of your feelings here, but this man is injured and it is our Christian duty to help him. I can't do it alone. I need your help. Please." I used some of the Cistercian guilt tactics I had learned from the brothers.

Robard was unmoved.

"Robard. Please. God is watching us," I said. Such a powerful weapon guilt can be. That should sway him. I hoped.

Robard puffed out his cheeks, letting out a sigh full of indignation and annoyance. But slinging his bow over his shoulder he walked to where I knelt holding the Assassin about the shoulders.

"If you hold him up, I will see to the arrow," I said.

Robard and I switched places. With my fingers I probed the tissue around the wound, and when I took the arrow firmly in my hand and began moving it about, the Assassin's eyes flew open and he bellowed out in pain. With his good arm he grabbed at my hands, shouting at me in Arabic.

"Watch out!" shouted Robard. "He . . ."

"Hold!" I hissed, grabbing the Assassin's arm. He stopped yelling momentarily.

I held up the stick so he could see it. I mimed putting the stick in my mouth and biting down on it. The Assassin looked down at his wound, then at me again, nodding. I held out the stick and he took it between his teeth.

Trying to still my shaking hand, I clutched the arrow firmly by the shaft. The Assassin took a deep breath and held it. I pushed gently on the arrow at first, hoping to work it through easily, but it was not to be.

I looked at the Assassin, who nodded again, closing his eyes. I tightened my grip on the arrow, pushing harder.

The Assassin screamed through his clenched lips, and his body straightened and tensed. I felt the arrow go in farther, but it was still stuck. I shifted my weight, pushing down still harder, and the Assassin shrieked in pain. Slowly the arrow began to move, but the Assassin was thrashing and kicking, and it was difficult to keep my grip.

"Hold him!" I hissed.

Robard gripped the Assassin more tightly by the shoulders, and I pushed again. The Assassin's body was nearly rigid. He bellowed, wiggling and kicking his legs, but at last I felt the arrow exit through the skin on his back with a pop and the arrowhead came free. He threw back his head, letting loose one final cry, then passed out.

Robard looked up at me, his face a mass of confusion. At first, I didn't notice because I was busy wiping the sweat from my forehead and trying to pull myself together.

"Tristan," Robard whispered. "Look."

I followed Robard's gaze to the face of the Assassin. During all the thrashing and kicking about, the Assassin's turban had been knocked loose and the veil had fallen away. Only it wasn't *his* face. It was *her* face.

For before us, lying there in Robard's arms, was not the hardened visage of a determined killer. Instead, there was the almost innocent face, framed by long, flowing and beautiful black hair, of a young girl.

The Assassin was a she.

23

Her hair was the color of obsidian. She looked young, perhaps fifteen or sixteen. She had fallen unconscious again, and Robard held her stiffly at the shoulders, as if any movement on his part might cause her to break. Clearly he had no idea what to do with her. I was too stunned to move or speak. Perhaps this explained why her companions had run off. If they were all as young as she, they likely were not experienced fighters.

Finally Robard broke the silence. "Tristan! It's a girl!" he said, his voice a whisper.

"I can see it is a girl, Robard."

"I've never heard of a female Assassin," he said.

"Nor have I."

We were silent again, our eyes transfixed on the face of the girl before us. The sky was getting darker, but I could see her face was pale and not her natural color. She had sharp cheekbones, but a small rounded nose, and her thick hair smelled of sandalwood.

"Tristan," Robard said quietly.

"Yes," I answered, not looking up from the face of the girl.

"Perhaps you should finish with the arrow. She's still bleeding," he said.

Robard's words snapped me out of my reverie. "Can you hold her up? I need to see her back now."

Robard complied, moving to the other side of her prone body. I could see where the arrowhead had come through, slightly beneath her shoulder blade. The arrowhead was attached to the shaft with a length of leather twine. I cut through it with my knife, and the arrowhead popped off onto the ground.

With the point removed it was much simpler to pull the shaft free of her shoulder. Simpler perhaps, but not without pain. When I pulled it free of her body, she stiffened, letting out a pitiful moan. But it was out. I cut a section from the fabric of her tunic and fashioned a bandage, which Robard helped me secure tightly around her shoulder.

"We need to take her with us," I said.

"What?" He was incredulous. "You can't be serious."

"I'm completely serious. She is wounded and in our care. It wouldn't be right to leave her. She could die here alone," I said.

I could tell from the look on Robard's face that he had no problem leaving the Assassin behind. He stared at me a moment. "You are a strange one, Tristan, squire of the Templars," he said.

"Yes. Well. We need to make a litter to carry her," I said, drawing my short sword and offering it hilt first to Robard. "Can you take my sword and cut two saplings, strong enough to hold her, about six feet in length?"

Robard made no move, merely staring at me a moment. Then he seemed to come to terms with something and nodded, taking my sword and exiting the camp.

The girl was still unconscious. I built a small fire, figuring it would be safe since we were well hidden from the road. Besides, anyone drawn to it meaning us harm would have to contend with an angry King's Archer before relieving us of our possessions.

In the woods nearby I picked some waxroot. Back at the fire, I shaved the roots of the plant into small slivers, filled my cup with water and heated it on the fire. While it warmed, I gathered up everything from the campsite, including the Assassin's daggers, and packed them away.

Eventually she began to stir, groaning in pain a few times. Her eyes opened, and with her good arm, she struggled to push herself into a sitting position. She began to wail, chanting something in Arabic, and I didn't know what she was saying, but I heard fear in her voice.

Robard returned from the woods carrying the two saplings I'd asked for.

I held up my hands to her, palms empty. "Please," I said. "Do not move. Quiet now. It will be all right." I kept my voice calm and low.

She looked at me and fell silent as we appraised each other.

Slowly, I reached for the cup, lifting it in front of me. I held it out for her, but she did not take it. In fact her eyes grew narrow and suspicious.

"Please. Drink." I held the cup near my lips, then reached out with it again. She sat there as silent as a stone.

"She won't drink it unless you drink first," Robard said. "She thinks you might be trying to poison her. I've heard Assassins often use poisons to kill an enemy."

At the sound of Robard's voice, she turned to look at him, studying him intently for a moment before returning her gaze to me. While she watched, I took a long sip of the waxroot tea, then held the cup out to her again.

Finally she sat up straight, reaching for the cup with her good arm. She took a small sip. The tea was bitter and she made a face at the taste, but I held up a sprig of the plant as she drank, hoping she would recognize it and realize what the tea was made from. She nodded and drank again.

We were silent while she drank her tea. When she finished, she handed me the cup and lay back down on the ground. I added more limbs to the fire, and in a few minutes she had fallen fast asleep again.

While she slept, I removed my tunic, turning it inside out so the sleeves were inside the garment. I pushed the saplings through the armholes. By tying the front of the tunic closed I created a very crude stretcher. It should hold the Assassin long enough for us to get away safely.

I sat it on the ground next to the sleeping girl, motioning for Robard to help me lift her onto the stretcher. Surprisingly he did so without complaint, and when we had her nestled safely there, we each picked up our end and carried her out of the campsite and into the woods.

We had delayed our departure long enough. Her companions could return at any moment with a larger force. We took off at a slow trot, heading east. For the first few minutes the girl whimpered in pain as she bounced along on the litter. After a while, though, her cries ceased and she fell unconscious again.

We didn't speak or stop to rest. It was difficult to make good time. Robard had taken the front, and as he ran, I heard him mutter under his breath. Words and phrases like *crazy plan* and *stubborn* and *what am I doing* filtered back to me on occasion.

After running for nearly an hour, I estimated we had traveled three leagues. We stopped to rest. I had some figs and dates in my satchel, and Robard and I wolfed them down hungrily. We were breathing hard and sweat was streaming off our faces. For a moment I wondered if we were doing the right thing. Would Sir Thomas or Sir Basil do as I had done? In enemy territory where silence and stealth is of the utmost importance, would they crash loudly through the woods to carry a wounded enemy to safety? After thinking on it a moment I realized that yes, they would have.

Robard knelt a few paces away, scanning the trail ahead of us. I took the water skin to him and offered him a drink.

"Tristan, I'm not sure how much longer I can keep going. This is dangerous. With the noise we're making and the fact that we won't be able to draw a weapon until we put down the litter, we're at a big disadvantage. Anyone, bandits or Assassins, could be upon us before we even know it," he said.

I knew Robard was right, but I still felt that we needed to make sure the Assassin was well enough before we left her behind.

"How much longer until we reach Tyre, do you think?" I asked.

Robard shrugged.

Then a voice from behind us said, in perfect English, "Well, since you're headed in the completely wrong direction, I'd say never."

t the sound of the voice I was so startled I visibly jumped in the air. Robard let out a gasp and fumbled at his bow, but when we turned at the sound, we saw the girl standing behind us, her wounded arm held loosely at her side.

We stared, dumbstruck. Though pale and somewhat unsteady on her feet, she otherwise seemed well enough.

"Who are you?" Robard asked, not quite sure what to do. The look on his face was comical. My hand had flown to the hilt of my sword at the sound of her voice. Now I felt ridiculous and dropped it to my side.

"I am Maryam," she said, looking at me. "Your name is Tristan, correct?"

I nodded.

"I thank you for tending to my shoulder. It is painful and will be for a while, but I appreciate your efforts," she said.

"It was nothing," I answered.

"I helped," Robard said. I shot Robard a glare. If helping constituted complaining and gathering water, then yes, he had helped.

"Yes, and thank you as well," she said, looking at him.

She spoke perfect English, apparently able to understand us the entire time she had been conscious.

"How is it you speak English?" I asked.

"I come from a small village near Jerusalem. My father owned a farm nearby, and we traded there when Christians occupied the city. It was necessary to learn English to make a living," she said.

Robard and I were unsettled. First we were attacked. Then we discovered that one of the attackers was a girl. Next we learned she spoke English. What next?

"Why are you headed to Tyre?" she asked.

I had no intention of telling her the true nature of my mission. Or even that I carried dispatches for the Templar Commandery there. She was an enemy after all. I decided to use Robard's excuse, glancing at him first and tilting my head, hoping he was wise enough to play along. "We are hoping to find a ship to England. Our conscription is over," I said. Robard nodded in agreement, understanding the need for a ruse.

Maryam looked at me a moment as if she didn't quite believe me, but did not press it.

Now that she was standing, the color was slowly returning to her face. Her hair cascaded around her shoulders, glimmering in the moonlight.

"I helped," Robard reminded her.

She laughed. It sounded like music. "Thank you, Archer, even though it was your lucky shot that hit me," she teased. She appeared to bear him no ill will for having wounded her in the first place.

Robard's eyes narrowed. He was not quite sure what to make of her. He muttered under his breath, but the phrase *lucky shot, my arse* stood out.

"How did you find us in the woods?" I asked.

She looked at me, then stared off, either not knowing or not wanting to say.

"I'm not sure. We were patrolling. Ahmad, our leader, saw the boulders and thought that it might make a good hiding place for enemies. He spotted you and ordered an attack," she said.

I wondered then if she was lying. Her explanation didn't make sense. There were dozens of outcroppings of boulders in the area. Out of all of them they had stumbled across ours? Had we made some mistake? Her answer seemed vague, and I wondered if we had accidentally revealed ourselves somehow. Did she hope we might make the same mistake again, leading her companions directly to us?

"Why were you sleeping in the daytime? Why travel at night?" she asked.

"We thought it safer. This area is full of bandits as well as Saracen patrols. And Assassins, as we've learned. With just the two of us we thought it better to travel by night."

She accepted my explanation with a nod. "Well, shall we get started?" she asked.

"Get started? What do you mean?" Robard asked.

"To Tyre, of course."

Robard coughed and asked to speak to me privately. We ventured a few paces away.

"Tristan, I can understand you treating her wounds. I can even understand carrying her to safety, but we cannot trust her. She's an *Assassin* for heaven's sake! What if she's leading us into a trap? She seems well enough to travel alone now. I say we leave her and make our way to Tyre on our own," he said.

I was quiet for a moment, trying to think. Perhaps Robard was right. It was time to take our leave.

We ambled back to Maryam.

"Maryam, I . . . we appreciate your offer, but since you seem well enough to travel, Robard and I think we will move on alone from here. Thank you though," I said.

Maryam looked at us a moment, then smiled and laughed.

Robard grew a little hot under the collar. "What's so funny?" he asked.

"Nothing. Except that you are heading directly *away* from Tyre now. If you got lost so easily, what makes you think you'll be able to find it on your own?" she said.

In all the excitement, I had momentarily forgotten that Maryam had informed us that we had been traveling in the wrong direction.

Robard's cheeks turned red. "We knew that. We were merely taking a slightly easier path since we had to carry you," he said.

"Hmm. Really? It just looks like you might want someone to guide you there," she said.

"What? Why do you think we need to be led anywhere?" he sputtered.

"Because if you keep going this way, you'll run into a few regiments of Saracens," she said.

My stomach tightened and I felt a momentary surge of panic. Saracens nearby? Patrols, yes. Small units, perhaps, but whole regiments? This far east?

"How do you know that?" I asked.

"My patrol camped with them just two days ago. If you wish to avoid them, you need to head toward the coast. Stay inland like this and you'll be discovered for sure," she said.

"And just what makes you think they will discover us?" Robard asked.

"Well . . . we did, didn't we?" she said. From where I stood I could swear that her eyes twinkled as she said it.

Robard looked at me. His face was a mask of red. Not rage, but embarrassment. "Tristan? A moment?" He nodded for me to follow him.

We again stepped away where Maryam couldn't overhear us.

"Do you believe her?" he asked.

"I don't know."

"What if she's telling the truth though? About the Saracens?" he said.

I just shrugged.

"Although I suppose it's just as likely she could be deceiving us," he said.

There was much to consider. I remembered conversations I had overheard among the knights in Acre. They spent hours discussing strategy and tactics. King Richard wished to hold the coastal cities. From there he hoped to push inland, retaking Jerusalem. He could keep his supply lines open as he moved into the interior. However, he had already lost Acre. The Saladin was likely to move toward Tyre next. It would be a logical target. So, in fact, Maryam could be telling the truth. Saracen regiments could be nearby.

"I think she's telling the truth," I said.

"I'm not sure I trust her," Robard said.

"I know, but she knows this country better than us. She could be leading us into a trap, I suppose, but from what I know of

Assassins they are honorable warriors. She will be honor bound to us for saving her life," I said.

"That's taking a big risk," he said.

"Yes, but if there are that many Saracens nearby, then we need to get to Tyre as fast as we can to warn the Templars there."

Although Robard wasn't happy, he agreed. He may not have loved the King, but he still behaved like a soldier. He would do his duty. We returned to Maryam.

"We accept your offer. We will follow you to Tyre. Are you well enough to keep up?" I asked.

"Oh, I wouldn't worry about me," she said, smiling.

"Very well then. Let's get going." I picked up the litter and removed my tunic from the poles, tossing the saplings into the underbrush.

Slipping it back on, I was tying it about my waist when Robard hissed, "Do you hear that?"

From out of the darkness came the sound of approaching hoofbeats.

aryam and I froze. Ahead of us, Robard waved frantically, motioning us back the way we had come. With no clouds and the light of the half-moon, we could see well enough to pick our way back through the trees on the trail we'd just traveled. The sound of hoofbeats grew louder, but it was impossible to tell who might be about to ride down on us. It could be Saracens or Crusaders. We needed to make ourselves invisible.

Robard scurried back to us. "This way! Hurry," he whispered.

We followed Robard a few paces toward a small thicket. The bushes were dense and close to the ground. It would provide good cover. We wormed our way down through them until we lay on the ground, facing the clearing we'd just left.

Before long, a group of horsemen rode into view. Saracens. I felt my heart rise to my throat. It appeared to be a single detail of ten men. They reined to a stop and the leader of the group began talking to his second in command.

We lay still, not twenty yards from where the men sat astride their horses. Maryam lay between Robard and me, studying the men intensely. Robard had managed to draw an arrow and nock it in his bow, which was on the ground in front of him. He was ready to rise and shoot in an instant.

Moving my hand to the sword at my belt I managed to silently draw it while keeping it at my side. We barely dared to breathe.

"What are they saying?" Robard asked in a quiet whisper.

"The second in command is explaining that he heard voices here," Maryam whispered back.

"Shh!" I hissed. I wished them both quiet. This was no time for a conversation!

We watched the patrol as they talked, their horses prancing and whinnying, impatient to be under way again. After a moment, four of the men dismounted and began studying the ground. They each walked outward from the group in a different direction. I held my breath. If they discovered our tracks, they could follow them right to where we were concealed in the thicket. The half-moon was lower in the sky now as morning approached. It would make it difficult, but not impossible, to find our footprints. The men took their time, moving farther outward from the main patrol, which stayed mounted in the clearing.

I turned my head facedown into the ground so the moonlight would not reflect off my face, but still tried to keep an eye on the patrol. The four dismounted men were examining the bushes. To my dismay one of them headed straight for us. He walked slowly, looking carefully at the ground, his hand on the scimitar hanging at his belt. His eyes swept back and forth through the underbrush, and with each step he grew closer and closer to our position in the thicket.

Robard and Maryam were completely silent. The sound of my own blood thundered in my ears. In a few more seconds the Saracen would be upon us. I squeezed the hilt of my sword, certain that he must be able to hear my heart beating.

Slowly, agonizingly, he walked toward us. Then, when he was so close I could reach out and grab his ankle, I heard a low humming sound—the same sound that had awakened me as Maryam and the Assassins attacked us in the rocks. It was coming ever so softly from the satchel, which now lay on the ground beside me. I felt sickness rising in my stomach. Surely the Saracens would hear it and discover us. Robard and Maryam were still and soundless next to me. Out of the corner of my eye, I saw Maryam, and if she heard the sound, she did not acknowledge it.

The Saracen drew closer. He was standing less than a foot away from me. In our dark clothing and what little moonlight there was, we blended in well with the ground cover. I tensed, expecting to feel the thrust of a scimitar at any moment.

The Saracen stood still. From the angle now I couldn't see his face, only his feet. Surely he must be looking directly at us. Yet he remained motionless as the seconds crept by.

At a sharp order in Arabic from his leader, the Saracen turned on his heel, returning to the clearing. After a few more minutes of talk, the men remounted and rode off.

I let out a breath and felt like I might faint. We waited for several minutes, making sure they didn't return. When enough time had passed, and the night sounds of the forest began again, we crawled our way out of the thicket. Robard returned the arrow to his wallet, and I sheathed my sword. I waited there a moment, bent at the waist with my hands on my knees, trying to relax myself. I had no idea how the Saracen had not discovered us.

"Did you hear that?" I asked, referring to the humming noise coming from the satchel.

"Hear what?" Robard asked.

"That noise . . . It sounded like . . . Never mind," I said.

This was the second time I'd heard the noise, both times when I was in physical danger. But I had no wish to explain it. I couldn't reveal how I had come to possess this thing I carried. I had lost my desire for that, at least for now. Robard was busy scanning the woods, apparently forgetting all about my question. For the time being, I let the matter drop.

"We must get moving," said Maryam, an intense expression on her face.

She trotted off, heading north toward the coast. We followed quickly after her, without speaking. Before long the woods began to thin and I smelled salt air. The terrain grew rockier, slowing our pace somewhat. Finally, we crested a rise, and below us lay the sea. The half-moon was now barely visible over the horizon, and its light gave a blue shimmer to the surface of the water. It was beautiful, and had I not been so worried at the thought of Saracen patrols all around us, I might have taken time to enjoy it.

We had been running for a while, but Maryam did not even stop to take in the sight of the glimmering water below us. She immediately turned east and continued racing along the ridge.

Finally, Robard called out that we needed to stop for a moment. We halted near a rocky outcropping and leaned against the boulders, breathing fast. The wind had picked up, and the night air was cooler nearer the coast. Robard drank from the water skin and passed it to me.

"We can't rest long," Maryam said. "We need to keep moving."

"Why?" Robard asked suspiciously.

"Because, *Archer*, where there is one Saracen patrol, there are many. We were nearly spotted once. Our best chance to reach Tyre is to keep moving."

Maryam was breathing hard, and the fading moonlight revealed that her face was flushed and damp.

"Maryam, are you feeling okay?" I asked.

"I'm fine," she said, "but we need to go."

"You seem in quite a hurry," said Robard. "Is there something you aren't telling us?"

"Robard . . . ," I said.

This time though, Maryam didn't answer, but merely handed me the water skin and took off running again along the ridge.

Robard and I trotted after her.

"Something is wrong," he said. "She heard those men say something. She's not telling us everything."

"We don't know that, Robard. She may just be trying to get us to Tyre as quickly as possible," I said.

"Yes. Remind me of that again when we are hanging in chains from the wall of the Saladin's prison," he said.

"Robard, do you see a conspiracy behind every tree? Is the entire world aligned against you?" I asked.

"Not the entire world," Robard answered.

We caught up to Maryam before long and continued running in silence. The moon set and the sky lightened to the east. It would be daybreak soon.

"I think we should stop," I said. "Without the cover of darkness, we are too exposed. We should find a place to camp for the day and continue tonight."

"We don't have time to stop," Maryam said. "We must keep going."

Her statement brought Robard and me to a stop. Maryam continued running.

"Wait," I hissed.

She stopped and turned.

"Why? Why can't we stop?" I asked. "I think you owe us an explanation."

Maryam paused. She looked at the ground for a moment. Then at me.

"Tristan, did I not make a promise to you that I would see you safely to Tyre?" she asked.

"Yes."

"I will keep that promise, but we must keep moving," she said.

"Why is that? What did you hear those men say?" Robard asked.

Maryam paused for a moment, glancing back and forth at us. She sighed.

"You're right, Archer. I did hear something. They were arguing about whether to continue to look for us or rejoin their forces," she said.

"So?" Robard said.

"The commander said that they needed to return to the main camp before the attack begins," she said.

"What attack? That could mean anything. There is plenty of fighting going on to the south and west," Robard said.

But I knew what attack the commander was referring to. "They're going to attack Tyre," I said.

Maryam was quiet and Robard looked at me.

"What? You don't know that," he said.

The look on Maryam's face told me I was right.

"There is not just one regiment nearby," she said. "There are more than thirty. With more arriving. They'll begin moving units toward Tyre in the morning."

It was just as I'd feared. The Saladin was moving quickly toward Tyre.

"How do we know she's telling the truth?" Robard said. "Stop a minute, Tristan. Perhaps she wants us to think that Tyre will be attacked while the real attack happens elsewhere."

"We can't take a chance on whether it's true or not. Knights in Acre discussed this many times. If the Saladin takes Tyre, the main road to Jerusalem and the interior is lost. King Richard will be forced to move even farther east and will not be able to resupply his forces on the plains. Maryam is right. We can't wait. We must get to Tyre and find the Templar Commandery. We must warn them," I answered.

"Have you even considered that she could be part of this?"

Maryam laughed. "Let me see if I understand you, Archer. By your way of thinking, I am a spy, privy to all of the Saladin's plans. To make his elaborate scheme work, I and my Hashshashin brothers leave our encampment and find you in the woods. During the attack I manage to get myself severely wounded, knowing in advance that my intended victims will nurse me back to health. When I am well enough, I promise to repay my debt to you and see you safely through Saracen lines to Tyre, but in reality it is all a ruse to provide

188

false information to the Christian commanders in the city, and then deliver you as prisoners to the Saladin himself. Does that about sum it up?" She looked at Robard and her obsidian eyes blazed, glinting in the moonlight.

Robard's face clouded, and he moved until his face was just inches from hers. She did not flinch.

"Excuse me for assaulting your tender sensibilities, but we only just met you. You tried to kill us. And I shot you," he reminded her. "You could be setting us up . . ."

Maryam's anger flashed across her face. "It was a lucky shot!" she said.

"It was not a lucky shot!" he shouted.

I cut in. "Robard, it doesn't matter anymore. There are Saracens within a few days' ride of Tyre. If we wish to make our way home, we must get there quickly and find a ship before we are trapped."

"I still think she's lying about something," he said.

"She isn't," I said. "Let's go."

Maryam looked at me in gratitude. I understood what she had done. She had promised to get us safely to Tyre. With the city under siege she knew we'd not be able to get home. She had shown me that her oath meant something to her.

As we ran, I thought about how just a short while ago we were cowering in a thicket, a few feet away from a detachment of Saracens. Lying there exposed, outnumbered, with nowhere to run if we were discovered. She could have easily betrayed us, but she had kept her word.

At least for now.

THE CITY OF TYRE

26

We ran through the remaining night. As morning approached, the sun entered the eastern sky slowly, as if it were reluctant to start the day. Our course held us fast along the coast, and as we ran, we could still glimpse the sea below us. White shorebirds began their morning rituals, diving and floating above the gentle swells cresting along the shore. On the gusting wind, I occasionally heard their songs as they twisted and darted over the water. I felt I was running through Eden itself. Looking at the gorgeous land before me, the water a stunning blue against the morning sky, the cliffs so stark in their beauty, I could scarcely believe this place had seen so many centuries of war and unrest. It felt peaceful beyond compare.

I had often wondered these past few months if all the fighting, killing and destruction had been worth it. Kings had been born and died here. Armies had fought here hundreds of years ago and fought again today. Battlefields had been taken and lost. Despite all that had happened in this place, the land itself was untouched by it. It remained peaceful and beautiful, as if it could speak to us. As if to say, "Fight on all you wish. I will not change. I am constant."

Two days of nearly constant running drew us ever closer to Tyre. As Maryam insisted, we ran through the daylight hours, and each morning as the sun took full effect and the temperature rose, I felt exposed, traveling out in the open as we were. I argued that we should move inland if we were to continue on this way. Maryam disagreed, countering that the woods were full of Saracens moving about and that we could stumble across a patrol or encampment at any moment. Running along the coast, at least we would see anyone coming from quite a way off. Then we could climb to the shore below us and hide among the rocks. This time Robard agreed with Maryam.

So on we ran. I had no idea how close we were to Tyre, but I felt it couldn't be much farther. If we had been traveling on the road, I think we would have begun seeing merchants and traders and other traffic heading to the city. Or perhaps the road would have been full of Saracens. Running on the open shoreline it felt as if we were the only people in the world. I knew that the nearer we drew to Tyre, the closer the main road would come to the shore, because the city sat right on the coast. At that point perhaps we would try to blend in with the traffic on the road and make our way to the city unnoticed.

Not knowing what lay ahead, I suggested we stop for a moment to check over our weapons. Robard tended to his bow while I examined my swords. Given the fact that Maryam had remained truthful thus far, I decided to return her daggers. As I fished them from my bedroll, I noticed how beautiful they were. The blades were polished to a high sheen, and the hilts were made of gold and bejeweled. They must have been worth a great deal.

I handed them to Maryam hilt first. She looked at them briefly, then, almost faster than I could see, flipped them around and secreted them in the sleeves of her tunic. Robard looked at me with wide eyes. I was glad Maryam was on our side. At least temporarily.

Well past noon we crested another ridge, and there in the distance lay Tyre. The sky was crystal clear, and I could see smoke from fires, ships moving in and out of the harbor, and all the other signs of life in a city. It was perhaps three leagues away, and indeed the main road emerged out of the hills to the south, leading straight to the city gates.

I suggested that we cut inland to the road. We were less likely to be noticed than if we approached the city along the shore. Robard and Maryam agreed and we headed south. Before long we had reentered the woods and soon had the road in sight. We paused, hiding in the underbrush and watching what passed by before we continued. For all we knew, Tyre could already be under the Saladin's control.

For an hour we watched and observed. Traders and merchants passed. Goatherds and shepherds with flocks of sheep moved along the road. When at last a squad of soldiers rode by, clearly members of the King's Army, we knew we were at least temporarily safe. As we had drawn nearer to Tyre, Maryam had restored her veil and turban. Moving from our hiding place she removed it. Her long black hair now cascaded down her shoulders and back. Robard and I were startled to see her like this again.

"I think Al Hashshashin might not be welcome in Tyre," she said. "It's better if I look like a simple peasant girl on my way to the marketplace. Don't you think?" She tucked in the hood of her tunic so it didn't show. Without the hood, turban and veil, her tunic transformed her from a Hashshashin and she looked much less dangerous than she actually was.

"A simple peasant girl with two Hashshashin daggers hidden in her sleeves who also happens to be a deadly killer. Sure," said Robard.

I expected Maryam to be angry, but instead she laughed. Again, her laughter was as joyous as the first time I'd heard it.

We crept cautiously from our hiding place onto the road. With no one immediately about we began walking quickly toward the city, entering Tyre a short time later without incident.

Tyre was bustling and loud, reminding me somewhat of Dover. But its marketplace was larger and more crowded, with a curious mix of new smells: cooking meat, the ocean, spices and incense, the earthy smells of camels and a thousand other scents I could not identify. It was hot in the afternoon sun, and the merchants and shopkeepers did everything they could to remain in the shade.

"What now?" Robard asked.

"I need to find the Templar Commandery immediately," I answered. "Then locate the Marshal and deliv . . . and talk to him about what we've seen." I glanced at Maryam, worried that I might have given something away, but her expression was blank. Although I felt at this point I could trust her, I did not wish to tempt her Hashshashin nature.

"Well, how do we find the Commandery?" Robard asked.

"I don't know. It should be easy to spot. They'll have the banner flying. There was supposed to be a large force here. Perhaps we should split—"

Maryam interrupted me. "Oh, for the grace of Allah," she snorted. "Why don't you just ask for directions?" Rolling her eyes she stomped up to a vendor at a nearby stall, speaking to him in Arabic. He answered her, pointing over his shoulder.

"This way," she said.

"Wait, Maryam," I said. "You have delivered us safely to Tyre as promised. You've fulfilled your obligation. Robard and I can take it from here."

Maryam looked at me and then Robard. She studied his face for several seconds.

"Well, I can accompany you to the Commandery at least. I don't mind. Besides, you may need me to translate for you if you get lost," she said.

With no time to argue, I agreed.

The marketplace at Tyre was a maze. The pathways through it twisted and turned, weaving through the rug merchants, food sellers and other stalls and shops. At every one of them, someone hollered at us to purchase something. I stopped at one point to buy each of us a lamb skewer, which a man sold hot off the fire. We devoured the meat in an instant, as we had hardly had time to eat in the previous two days.

Continuing to walk, I tried to organize my thoughts. I needed to inform the Templars of the impending attack. They would contact the King's military advisers and formulate a strategy. I would also inform them of the fall of Acre, if they hadn't already received word. Then I needed to find passage on a ship to England. But I must be careful. Sir Thomas had warned me that even Knights of the Temple had gone nearly mad trying to possess the Grail.

Passing through the marketplace we found a cobblestone street leading toward the eastern edge of the city. Maryam said the Commandery was not too far away now, and for some reason, the closer we got, the more nervous I became. As we passed an alleyway leading between two large buildings, I had a thought.

"Can both of you wait here a moment?" I asked. "I need to find a place to, well, you know . . ."

Robard laughed, and he and Maryam nodded. I headed down the alley. It wasn't straight, curving back and forth the farther along it I went. Finally I reached a quiet spot, glancing around and seeing no one about. Above me clothing dried in the sun on a line tied between the two buildings. A few empty barrels were stacked next to a door that led into the rear of one of the structures. A small yellow dog lay in the brief shade of a doorway, but its eyes were mostly closed as it napped in the heat of the afternoon sun. The coast was clear.

Moving several feet down the alley from the doorway, I found my spot. Kneeling in the dirt, I used the small knife from my satchel to make a footlong scratch in the side of the building, very near the ground. I rubbed a handful of sand over the fresh scratch so that it was still visible but did not look newly made. With my knife I scooped out a hole in the sand directly below the mark on the wall.

I hesitated for a moment, wondering if I should take Sir Thomas' letter with me to the Commandery; I might need it to prove my identity. But I finally decided it was safer to keep it for some future point in my journey. It shouldn't be that difficult to convince the local Commandery of my identity.

I placed Sir Thomas' letter and ring at the bottom, and after removing all my other possessions from the satchel, and double-checking to make sure that I was not being watched, I lifted out the Grail and set it gently in the hole. Then I covered it all with sand, smoothing it out with my hands. I repacked my possessions and stood up, walking back and forth over the spot numerous times, scuffing my feet. When I was finished, it looked like it had never been dug up at all.

As I turned back, the small dog lifted its head to watch me. It yawned, stretching as I passed by, and I reached down to scratch it behind the ears. A scrawny dog, it appeared as if it hadn't had much to eat recently. Inside my satchel I had a few dates I had saved, and I tore one into smaller pieces, holding them out for the dog to examine. She hungrily snatched them up. I gave her the rest of what I had, and the little mutt licked my hand before dropping her head back down and drifting off to sleep.

Maryam and Robard were standing where I'd left them, fidgeting. I was sure they hadn't spoken a word to each other since I'd been gone. Robard was doing everything in his power to look at anything but Maryam.

"Thanks," I said. "Let's go."

We continued down the street, and before long, the Commandery appeared, a Templar banner hanging from the roof. The sight was comforting. I felt relieved to see something so familiar. The front gate to the grounds was guarded by a single sergeanto. Dust lined his face, and he sweated in the heat. His expression said he'd rather be anywhere but on guard duty.

"Maryam," I said. "I think this is where we should say good-bye."

Sadness flitted across her face, but then she nodded.

"Thank you for guiding us here. I hope that you will make it safely to wherever you are going next," I said.

"Good-bye, Tristan. Good-bye, Archer. I hope our paths will cross again sometime," she said.

I felt like I should say more, but I had no idea what. She looked at me expectantly, but then turned her gaze on Robard. No matter what she was, I no longer felt like she was my enemy. And I don't think Robard did either, although he was probably loath to admit it.

"Yes. Well. Good-bye. Nice knowing you. Thanks for not killing us while our backs were turned," he said.

To my surprise Maryam laughed. Her hand darted out, and she briefly squeezed Robard on the forearm. Robard's face turned red at her touch, and he was suddenly consumed by a coughing fit.

With a smile Maryam turned and strolled off down the street.

Robard and I watched her go, then turned toward the guard.

"State your business," he ordered as we approached.

"I am Tristan of St. Alban's, squire to Brother Knight Sir Thomas Leux of the Dover Commandery most recently deployed in Acre. I have a report for the Marshal," I answered.

"I know of Sir Thomas, but I don't know you. Do you have proof of this?" he asked.

"I do. I carry his sword," I said, turning so the sergeanto could see the battle sword that I carried across my back. I also showed him the Templar seal carved into the hilt of my short sword. The sergeanto nodded but wasn't completely satisfied.

"Who is this?" he asked, pointing to Robard.

"This is Robard Hode, formerly of the King's Archers. He has accompanied me from Acre. Please, sergeanto, we saw Saracen patrols not more than a day away. I have urgent news for the Marshal. May we enter?"

His eyes flew open when I mentioned the nearby Saracens. He considered us a moment longer, then stepped aside and opened the gate.

"You will find the Marshal in the office off the meeting room in the main hall," he said.

This Commandery was quite similar to the one in Dover, with only minor differences in the construction of the buildings. It was made of mud bricks and once inside smelled like wet dirt, but the layout was almost identical.

Entering the main hall, it felt unusually quiet. I was used to the hubbub of the barracks and grounds in Acre, but perhaps the knights were off on patrols or performing other duties. A squire sitting at a table mending a harness directed us to the Marshal. He pointed to the left where a corridor led away from the main hall.

There was a small room at the end of the corridor, and as we approached, I could see through the doorway a man, dressed in a Marshal's tunic, sitting at a wooden table writing on parchment. A sergeanto stood next to him holding several more sheets, waiting for the Marshal's signature.

I knocked on the doorway.

"Sire, I beg your pardon for the disturbance, but I bring news from Acre and the knights there," I said.

Both men looked up. The Marshal studied me for a moment. He was a small man, balding and round faced. His eyes were dark, and it looked like a permanent frown was etched on his face. As he regarded me, his face was expressionless, but I could see cunning in his eyes. Something told me to be careful with what I said.

"You may enter," he said.

Stepping before his desk, I was about to begin my report when a voice from the corner of the room interrupted me. "I was wondering when you would show up."

A voice, contemptuous and full of hate, that I would know any-

201

where. My knees trembled and the blood rushed through my ears, and for a moment I thought I might faint.

My eyes needed to see to be sure that my ears did not deceive me, so I turned to look and there he was, standing in the corner, near a window that bathed the room in soft light.

Sir Hugh.

27

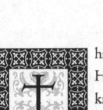his is the one I spoke of, Marshal Curesco," Sir Hugh said. His smile told me all I needed to know. It was a spider's smile, if spiders were to actually smile. He could barely contain his glee at finding me here. But how could this be? How could he have escaped from Acre? And more important, did he know what I carried here?

Sir Hugh's tunic looked freshly cleaned. He appeared fit and rested. True, he hadn't done much fighting in Acre, but now to see him up close, I was astounded to find him free of any signs of warfare or battle. No wounds or scars. Not a bruise to be seen. Just his pinched face and that same scraggly beard.

The Marshal looked at Sir Hugh, then at me. "Is that so?" he said.

"This one has been nothing but trouble since he joined the order. He has no doubt deserted his post in Acre, and it appears he has stolen Templar property."

"What? I have not stolen anything," I protested loudly.

"Then how do you explain this sword?" Sir Hugh strode across the room, drawing the sword that hung across my back. "This sword belonged to Sir Thomas Leux of my regiment. I would like to know how this boy has possession of it," he said.

Marshal Curesco looked at me, waiting for an answer.

"This is Sir Thomas' sword, that is true. But he gave it to me when I left Acre. Under his orders." I turned, staring directly at Sir Hugh when I spoke. He didn't hold my gaze, walking around behind the table to stand at Marshal Curesco's side, opposite the other knight.

"And why did he order you away from Acre, exactly?" the Marshal asked.

"The Saladin's forces breached the city walls. We fought hand to hand through the city. The knights prepared to make a last stand in the Crusaders' Palace. There is a secret passage there. Sir Thomas sent me through it with orders to travel to Tyre as quickly as I could and deliver the news. I met up with Robard a few days' journey from Tyre and we traveled here together," I told him.

The Marshal's eyes narrowed and he leaned back in his chair, trying to take it all in.

"When did you leave Acre?" he asked.

"More than a week ago. Sir Thomas gave me strict instructions to travel only at night. That slowed me down. We had some encounters with bandits, but managed to run them off." I didn't mention the Assassins. No sense in giving out too many details.

"This is absurd," Sir Hugh cried. "He is obviously a liar and a thief. We should throw him in the jail immediately!"

Marshal Curesco held up his hand, silencing Sir Hugh.

"Do you have anything that proves your story?" Marshal Curesco asked.

For a moment I regretted leaving Sir Thomas' ring and letter hidden with the Grail. But instinct had commanded me, and no doubt Sir Hugh would have accused me of stealing the ring as well.

"Just this. If I am the thief Sir Hugh thinks I am, why would I bother to come straight here to the Commandery and report to you, with my 'stolen' sword so plainly in sight? Why would I not just slip away?"

Marshal Curesco glanced at Sir Hugh and seemed on the verge of considering my argument.

"And there's one more thing, another reason why I came immediately here. A few days ago we narrowly escaped detection by a patrol of Saracens."

Marshal Curesco immediately leapt to his feet. "Saracens? Are you certain?" he asked.

Throughout this entire exchange, Robard had remained silent in the corridor behind me. He decided now was the time to speak up.

"Of course we're certain. I've been fighting them nonstop for the last two years. I think I know what a Saracen looks like," he offered. And for added effect he looked directly at Sir Hugh, as if sensing his natural cowardice, and said, "Do you?"

Sir Hugh glared at Robard but said nothing.

"And where were you? Exactly?" the Marshal asked.

"Not more than forty leagues west of the city. We heard a patrol approaching and managed to hide in the underbrush. They searched for us for a while but then gave up when their commander ordered them to remount. He said they needed to return to camp to ready for the attack on Tyre," I said.

"And how do you know what a Saracen commander said?" Sir Hugh cut in.

I realized my mistake. I couldn't tell them about Maryam. If I did, they'd never believe me. I needed a convincing lie.

"We were camped with a trader, bound for Tyre. He spoke Arabic, and he heard the Saracens' words." Every time I told a lie, the abbot's face popped into my head. He would be disappointed in me for all the lies I had learned to tell so easily. A small bead of sweat found a path from my forehead down my cheek. The look on the Marshal's face was impossible to read. Did he believe me?

"Marshal Curesco, he is lying. He is trying to concoct some story of an attack to cover up his crimes! I demand we put him in jail right now!" Sir Hugh was obviously excited at the prospect of seeing me in chains.

Marshal Curesco turned to the sergeanto standing beside him.

"Brother Lewis, please gather a few men-at-arms and escort these young men to the jail. Hold them until I return from the King's headquarters. We will sort this out later. If indeed there are Saracens nearby, we will need to discuss our strategy," he said.

Brother Lewis shouted out a command, and I heard the corridor behind me fill with men-at-arms.

"What?" Robard yelled. "You'll not lock me away!"

He began pushing his way down the hallway, but the men-at-arms blocked his path.

I turned back to Marshal Curesco.

"Marshal Curesco! You cannot do this. I am telling you the truth! Please!" I pleaded.

"That may be. But I cannot discount the word of another Marshal of the Order. I promise you that you will be held there only until I return from conference with the King. We must attend to this news of the Saracens. Then we will sort out the facts of your story," he said.

Sir Hugh glared at me, but his lips curled into a self-satisfied smile. I knew we would never see Marshal Curesco again if Sir Hugh had his way.

The men-at-arms led Robard out of the hallway. They had relieved him of his bow and wallet. Two others entered the room and relieved me of my short sword, each taking an arm and leading me toward the corridor.

"Sire, please!" I shouted, struggling against their grip. But Marshal Curesco was already talking busily with Brother Lewis. He gave me a dismissive wave.

We were led out of the main hall and through the gates of the Commandery past the startled guard who had let us enter only moments before. Robard was shouting and cursing, making a very big commotion, but with no weapon there was little he could do. The men-at-arms ignored him.

"So, it would appear that your protector has abandoned you," Sir Hugh said tauntingly.

"Sir Thomas has likely died a hero's death, fighting with his comrades to the end. Unlike you, who seem to have made a very convenient escape from an embattled and surrounded city. How did you do it? How did you flee Acre?" I asked.

"My activities are no concern of yours," he said. "I can't tell you how it pleases me to see your fall from grace. Sir Thomas was an officious, pompous fool. Countermanding my orders in front of the men, doing anything he could to undermine and embarrass me . . ."

"You don't need anyone's help to embarrass yourself," I interrupted. Sir Hugh reacted by angrily shoving me forward into the street. I staggered but didn't fall.

"Well, it appears he misplaced his faith in you. Look at you

207

now. A failure easily captured and likely to hang, if I have anything to say about it. Which I will," he said.

I didn't respond, though I would certainly have voted against being hanged.

As we were dragged along toward the jail, small crowds of people formed in the streets to watch us pass by. For a moment I thought I saw Maryam. Here and there I caught a glimpse of a black tunic, but then I wasn't sure. It could have been anyone.

The jail was perhaps a half league from the Commandery, and shortly we entered a large earthen building. Inside was a single room holding a table and bench along the far wall to the right. Along the back wall were the cells—three of them built like cages in the room, each enclosed by iron bars, with a small barred window.

Our weapons were laid on the table. Robard was taken to the far left cell. The men-at-arms pushed him inside, shutting the door with a clang. Robard turned at the sound, spitting at them, cursing in very specific ways about what he thought of them and their mothers, but they paid him no mind.

"Now, young squire, you will answer my questions or you will spend the rest of your days in there," Sir Hugh said, pointing to the cell next to Robard. "Where is it? Do you have it with you?"

"Where is what?" I asked.

"Don't toy with me, squire," Sir Hugh said. "I give you marks for bravery, but now, tell me!" He ripped the blanket and satchel from around my shoulder. He walked to the table in the middle of the room, shaking out the blanket and dumping the contents of the satchel on the table.

"Where is it?" he snarled.

"I haven't any idea what you're talking about," I said.

"Do you think I'm joking, squire?" he sneered. His fist flew out and backhanded me across the face. I tasted blood in my mouth, but did not cry out.

Rubbing the blood from my lip, I vowed not to allow him to gain any advantage over me.

"What I *think* is that a nun hits harder than you. Other than that, I have no idea what you are talking about." Seeing Sir Hugh had started a fire in me again. I thought of Sir Thomas dying at his post. Then I saw this coward standing before me. He had slunk away before the last fight began, most likely. I could not bear it. Quincy and Sir Basil, some of the bravest men I knew, were likely dead, and this vermin thought he would break me? I swore that no matter what he did to me, I would tell this man nothing.

Sir Hugh's eyes bored into me, but I held his gaze, determined not to blink.

"You will tell me where it is. Now," he said.

"Sir Hugh, Sir Thomas sent me here to warn the Commandery that Acre had fallen. As I explained to the Marshal . . ."

Sir Hugh grabbed me by the tunic, pulling my face close to his. His voice was a whisper of barely contained rage.

"You have it. The Grail. Sir Thomas had it. He would not have left it in Acre. So he must have given it to you. I tell you so you understand me. *I* will have it! Now you will tell me where it is, do you hear me?"

"I'm sorry, what did you say?" I said to Sir Hugh, my face only inches from his mouth. His fist drew back again, but he stopped himself, releasing his grip on me as if some outside force had suddenly caused him to regain his composure. He rubbed his hands over his face, pacing back and forth before me a few times.

"All right, squire. You win. You have what I want. But I believe I possess something you will find far more valuable than the Grail."

"You have nothing I need, Sir Hugh," I said.

"Don't be so quick to judge, boy," he said.

He looked at me, his face almost gleeful, taking great joy in drawing out the moment. I waited, silent, determined not to let him bait me.

"I know who you are, where you were born, your parents, everything."

I tried not to let my face show anything, but failed miserably. I felt as if I'd been punched solidly in the stomach. My vision narrowed, and it was suddenly difficult to breathe. Then I remembered who I was dealing with.

"Liar. You lie," I said.

"No, I really don't," he said, his voice low enough so that only I could hear him. "I know everything, you see. We suspected you had been left at an abbey or a nunnery as a babe but weren't sure which one. We searched and searched for you for months after your birth, but the monks did a good job of keeping you hidden. Isn't it rich that I just stumbled across you fifteen years later? It was Sir Thomas who insisted that we stop at St. Alban's that night as we rode toward Dover. I thought nothing of it at first, but when you injured my horse and he took such an immediate interest in you, it aroused my suspicions.

"Interested now?" he asked, his face still only inches from mine. I said nothing.

"It took me a while, but I pieced it all together. I followed you to the stables that night intending to give you the thrashing you deserved. But that stupid monk showed up. Lucky for you. Then Sir Thomas invited you along with us and I knew there was more to you than met the eye. Sir Thomas would never take on such a doltish, incompetent squire.

"The next day I sent riders to the abbey. And I learned some interesting things," he gloated. I remembered seeing Sir Hugh with the King's Guards outside the Commandery gates. He had sent his men to the abbey? For what purpose?

"I learned a great many things. It's interesting what men will tell you when their fingers are being broken. Now I know everything, and I'll tell you everything. You just tell me where you've hidden the Grail. The knight you swore allegiance to has played you for a fool."

I felt dizzy and disoriented. I couldn't breathe. Sir Hugh had sent riders to the abbey to torture the monks and question them about me? Why? How could I possibly be that important? Now he claimed to have knowledge of the one thing I'd wished to know my entire life. Then Sir Thomas' words came back to me and I remembered the cretin who stood in front of me. A liar, a coward and a cheat. Even if I told him what he wanted, he would kill me anyway. I would need to find my answers elsewhere. He was probably lying about everything.

"No," I said. "I came here carrying news of Acre—"

Before I could finish, Sir Hugh bellowed in rage, grabbing my tunic in his fist and drawing his other hand back to strike me. Just then another man-at-arms burst into the room, saving me from another blow.

"Sir Hugh, Marshal Curesco has requested your presence at

the King's headquarters. We have other confirmed reports of Saracen patrols in the surrounding countryside. Battle orders are being drawn as we speak!" he said.

Sir Hugh's face paled at the mention of the Saracen patrols, his cowardice revealing itself again.

"Don't worry, Sir Hugh," I said. "There is still plenty of time for you to escape before the fighting starts."

Sir Hugh roared again, dragging me across the floor of the jail, then shoving me into the cell next to Robard. He glared at me and then straightened himself.

"Of course," he said to the newly arrived man. He pointed at the other two guards in the room. "Two of you stay here at all times. No one is to visit either of them. No one even enters this building without my orders. Understood?"

With a backward glance at me, Sir Hugh turned. "I'll return, squire," he hissed. "And when I do, I think you will tell me everything I want to know."

With that Sir Hugh and his men departed, leaving just the two guards for Robard and myself. I had no idea how to get us out of this mess.

To say Robard was in a state does not do justice to his mood. He paced back and forth in his cell like a caged beast, muttering and cursing. Finally he was quiet as he stared first at me, then at the men-at-arms sitting across the room.

"Care to explain?" he asked in a low voice.

I gave Robard a brief accounting of my history with Sir Hugh. "What I don't understand is how he escaped from Acre. The city was surrounded and overrun. The knights were making a last stand at the Crusaders' Palace," I said. I told Robard nothing of what Sir

212

Hugh had offered to tell me. No need to complicate things. Besides, I was sure he was lying anyway.

"Well, I have to tell you, I did not count on landing in a jail when I met up with you in the woods. I don't like this. I don't like this one bit," he said. He was angry. I held out my hands, waving them down, nodding toward the guards, who sat on a bench against the far wall. They looked bored and disinterested, but I had no doubt they'd been instructed by Sir Hugh to listen carefully to any conversation that passed between us.

"Robard, I am sorry you are caught up in this," I said. "I never expected to find Sir Hugh here alive. If the Templars perished defending Acre, he should be dead. Yet here he is. He must have found a way to sneak out of the city or else he took the same route I did."

But I knew why Sir Hugh was here. He wanted the Grail, plain and simple. What I could not figure out yet was how he knew I had it. Sir Thomas said only a few of the knights in the entire Order even knew of the Grail. He was one of the few, and I could not imagine him sharing that knowledge with Sir Hugh, whom he held in such low regard. Unless Sir Hugh knew of the Grail's existence before Sir Thomas did. Or had learned of its existence some other way and that Sir Thomas was the one who guarded it.

Something told me this was not the case. I couldn't imagine knowledge of something so valuable and rare being entrusted to such a liar and cheat. No doubt through villainous means, Sir Hugh had followed the trail that led to me. Now more than ever, I needed to find a way to get the Grail to safety.

Robard continued pacing. I moved to the corner of my cell and sat slumped against the wall. Soon the shadows grew darker and twilight crept in. When darkness arrived, one of the men-at-arms lighted an oil lamp sitting on the table, filling the room with dim light. Robard and I were silent for a long time, thinking.

"In the streets, as we were being led here, I thought I saw Maryam watching. Perhaps she'll . . ."

"Don't even mention her name," Robard interrupted. "She's under no obligation to help us anymore, anyway. She's long gone. If we're going to get out of here, we're going to have to do it on our own. We've seen the last of the Assassin."

With impeccable timing, Maryam's face appeared in the window of Robard's cell and she whispered quietly, "Hello, Archer. Did you miss me?"

28

he faint glow of the oil lamp gave us just enough light to see the dim outline of Maryam's face in the window. I was nearly speechless, and Robard stood frozen in place as if he'd seen a ghost.

"Don't stop pacing, you idiot! Keep moving like you were before or the guards will grow suspicious," she hissed.

Startled as he was, Robard resumed pacing back and forth, muttering under his breath. He threw a few curses and complaints at the guards for good measure.

"Tristan, I am about to create a diversion. Be ready!" she whispered.

"What? Wait . . . What are you going . . . ?" But she was gone before the words were out of my mouth.

For several minutes nothing happened. Robard continued pacing, and I sat slumped in the corner as if I were about to drift off to sleep. The guards still sat on the bench across the room, talking quietly.

The entrance to the jail had no door. It had either broken off or fallen into disrepair and been removed. A few minutes after

Maryam appeared in our window, we watched a smoking bundle of dried rushes come flying through the entryway, landing in the center of the room. They must have been coated in grease and dunked in water or mud, for instead of bursting into flames they merely created smoke, which began to fill the room.

The guards jumped to their feet, shouting. One ran to the center of the room, stomping at the bundle in an attempt to put out the sputtering flames. The smoke kept streaming off the rushes and he began coughing. Then two more torches flew in, landing at his feet. Smoke billowed up around him, and even in the dim light of the lamp he was almost invisible.

Both men were yelling now as the smoke thickened. It would soon reach our cell and we would not be able to breathe. The lamp on the table was suddenly extinguished, plunging the room into darkness except for a few flickering shadows cast by the flames of the torches. I heard a muttered curse, and then one of the guards let out a pained scream. I heard a sword being drawn, then the clang of steel followed by more curses and shouts.

Out of the commotion and noise, a shadowy figure appeared at my cell door, and a few seconds later it swung open. The figure moved to Robard's cell and his door opened as well.

"Come!" Maryam shouted. "This way!"

"Wait!" I called after her. I needed to get the satchel and my swords.

The smoke was disorienting, but I had a general sense of which direction to go. I couldn't see Maryam or Robard, but heard them moving toward the door. I quickly crossed the room toward the table holding our weapons and supplies. Halfway to where I thought the table should be, I stumbled over something on the floor, falling hard to the ground. It was one of the guards. He didn't move, and for a moment I worried that Maryam had killed him. But a groan escaped his lips and I realized he was only stunned. I scrambled to my feet, staggering the rest of the way across the room to the table. Feeling around with my hands, I grabbed the satchel, quickly throwing it over my shoulder.

I ran my hand over the table, finding my swords and gathering them up. I started moving toward the door, then remembered Robard's bow and wallet of arrows. Taking them as well as our bedrolls, I touched along the wall with my shoulder until I reached the door.

Robard and Maryam stood waiting just outside the door. It was good to breathe the cool night air. I handed Robard his bow and arrows, and we wasted no time running away.

Just a few yards down the street we heard the shouts of the guards as they emerged from the smoking jail. They hollered loudly, sounding the alarm, and we ran faster. Maryam led us down the street, turning at the first intersection. Sprinting until we reached the next alley we ran through it and then another, until the shouts of the guards faded away. Approaching the entrance to another street, we carefully peered out at a main thoroughfare lighted by torches every few yards. A few cooking fires still burned in the ovens and clay chimneys that stood in front of the buildings lining the street. We saw no one in either direction.

Looping Sir Thomas' battle sword over my back I hooked the short sword to my belt.

"Robard, I am sorry for what happened. I never expected to find Sir Hugh in Tyre," I said.

"We'll discuss it later. Let's escape first," he said.

"Agreed. Let's head for the docks. There will be taverns there, and where there are taverns there are sailors. We should be able to find passage on a ship. Sir Thomas left me with some money, enough to get us back to England. Maryam, can you take us there?" I asked.

"Yes, but we must hurry. Those guards will return to the Commandery and bring help. The docks are the first place they'll look. The city gates are closed at night, so we can't get out that way unless we climb the walls, which are guarded. Let's go," she said.

Maryam started down the street.

"Wait!" I yelled.

She stopped.

"I need to get something first. In the alley this afternoon I buried something. It's quite valuable and I must retrieve it. Can you lead us back there first?"

In the low light from the torches and fires I could see Robard's eyes narrow.

"I thought you told me you carried dispatches and orders for the Templars in Tyre," he asked.

"I did. I do. I am. Or was," I said. I had hoped he would not ask these questions.

"You gave nothing to the Marshal. Did you bury the orders? What did you have that you didn't want the Templars here to see?" he asked.

"It is a long story. Full of intrigue, with many layers," I exaggerated. "For now, let's just say that I was following orders. At the first opportunity I will explain everything. Now, however, I would suggest more escaping." I hoped I sounded convincing, but I also hoped

Robard would forget that I would explain later. I had promised Sir Thomas I would tell no one.

Robard's face held its puzzled expression, but then he shrugged.

"In case I haven't mentioned it, we need to hurry!" Maryam cut in. "If you wish to return to that alley, it's this way."

We set off at a brisk walk. Running would only attract attention, and we wished to be invisible. Crossing back through the now mostly deserted marketplace, I soon recognized the street we'd traveled along on the way to the Commandery earlier that day. We walked carefully through the stalls and carts, pausing now and then to make sure there were no men-at-arms or guards in the area. All was quiet.

A few minutes later we stood at the entrance to the alley.

"This is it," Maryam said.

The alley ran between two large stone buildings. Affixed to the wall of each building was a burning torch, giving light to the street where we stood. I took one of the torches and, holding it high in front of me, started off down the alley.

Everything seemed different in the darkness. The torch cast flickering shadows on the walls, and for a moment I was convinced that I was in the wrong place. At last I spotted the mark I'd scratched into the side of the building. I knelt, sticking the end of the torch into the ground, scooping away at the sand with my hands.

A few inches down, I uncovered the ring and Sir Thomas' letter. I stuffed them in the satchel and kept digging. Shoveling out more sand, then more, a sinking feeling began growing in the center of my gut. Frantically I clawed at the sand until I had made a very large hole. The Grail was gone.

Sitting back on my knees, I felt sick and light-headed. As impossible as it seemed, someone had found where I had hidden the Grail. But it made no sense. If they had taken the Grail, if they considered it valuable, why not take the ring as well? It would also fetch a handsome price. I was sure I'd placed the Grail on top of the ring and letter. Or had I? In a frenzy, I dug again at the hole, but it was no use. It was gone.

I sat there too stunned to move, realizing that I must have been followed. Or someone must have seen me in the alley. However it happened, I had been spotted burying the Grail, and someone had dug it up and it was gone forever. I had failed. I had given Sir Thomas my promise and I had failed.

Then I heard a growling sound behind me. It was a soft low sound, and it startled me. I grabbed the torch with one hand and jumped to my feet. My other hand flew to the sword at my belt. I turned around to see what else could go wrong in this truly remarkably bad day I was having.

A dog, the dog I had seen that afternoon, small and golden, stood in the alley. In its mouth it held the Grail still wrapped in linen. As I reached for it, the dog backed away, growling.

"Good girl. Nice dog. Give me the Grail, please?" I pleaded. I reached again, and the dog inched backward. I was running out of time. No matter what I tried, the dog refused to give up its prize. In desperation, I felt inside my satchel. In the bottom I found a piece of date that I'd missed earlier when I'd treated the dog. I pulled it out and offered it.

It slowly stepped forward and placed the Grail gently at my feet, swallowing the date in a single gulp.

elief washed over me as I reached down and clutched the Grail with both hands. The dog slowly rolled over on its back, its paws in the air, giving a small yip. I was nearly in tears, but I gave her a rub on the belly. I unwrapped the linen covering to make sure it was the same Grail I had seen a few nights ago, and offered up a prayer of thanks.

"Good girl," I said. The dog snorted and huffed, but clearly loved the belly rub. "Good girl." She licked my hand, then stood looking at me expectantly.

Dumping out the contents of the satchel I placed the Grail in the secret compartment. Scooping everything back inside, I grabbed the torch, heading back the way I'd come. The dog fell into step alongside me. I stopped.

"Stay, girl. You can't come with me."

The dog sat on its haunches looking at me expectantly. Her face was a mass of fluffy golden hair. Her kind, intelligent eyes were dark brown and never wavered from my own.

"I can't take you along, pup," I said.

I started up the alley and once more the dog trailed right along beside me. I stopped again and she promptly sat. I started. So did the dog.

"Girl, stay!" I said, trying to keep my voice down, but growing a little impatient.

I broke into a trot up the alley and she loped easily along at my side. Nothing I tried worked. It looked like I had gained another companion.

Robard and Maryam were right where I had left them, standing on either side of the alley, keeping an eye on the street. They both looked at me as I approached the alley entrance. Robard spotted the dog first.

"What is that?" he asked.

"A dog."

"I can see that! What are you doing with it?" he said.

"I believe it is more what she is doing with me," I answered. "I tried to get her to stay, but she seems convinced that she needs to come with us."

Robard snorted, but Maryam knelt, scratching the mutt behind the ears and laughing as the dog jumped at her, licking her face. It was the first time I had heard Maryam giggle like that.

"Any sign of Sir Hugh's men?" I asked.

"None," Robard replied.

"Let's get moving. We need to get to the docks," I said.

Maryam rose, and with no one in sight we moved out of the alley. She led us down a cobblestone pathway where we cut through another alley. Moving back and forth through the twisting, turning streets it was not long before I was horribly lost. The whole time the dog trotted along beside us, perfectly content to be in our company.

The city was quiet at night, but I heard the sounds of people as we passed by taverns and houses. Laughter and shouts escaped into the darkness, mixing with the spicy smells of cooking fires. It was a pleasant contrast to the busy activity during the daylight hours.

Finally we exited an alley and before us lay the waterfront. It was a shabby-looking place with a few decrepit buildings running directly along the shore. A long wooden dock jutted out into the water perpendicular to the street. A single longboat was moored to it. Out in the bay I saw several ships lying at anchor, bobbing gently in the moonlit waves.

Flashing back to my first sea voyage to Outremer, I did not relish getting on a ship again. My stomach lurched at the thought. But a ship would get me home faster and relieve me of the Grail. Taking the overland route would take months and was rife with danger. Added to that was the fact that I had no idea how to even find the overland route and my options were limited. I needed a ship.

"What now?" asked Maryam.

In reality, I had no idea. I had hoped to find the waterfront in the daylight hours. Then I could have taken a careful assessment of the ships in the harbor, asking people on the docks who might provide us with a good vessel at a fair price. Now our situation was more desperate. Undoubtedly we had Sir Hugh and his men-at-arms searching the city for us. It was imperative to find a ship that could leave immediately.

"We'll need to find a captain. My guess would be that we look there first." I pointed to a run-down, dilapidated old building standing a few yards away. Light came through the windows, and I heard the buzz of voices rising and falling inside. A sign hanging above the door said "The Dancing Fig" in English with some Arabic words written underneath. It did not look inviting. The door burst open and a man staggered out, stumbling a few steps before falling face-first in the dirt. He lay there moaning a few moments, then clambered to his feet. Letting out a mighty belch he wandered off down the street.

Robard and Maryam looked at the building, then at each other, then at me. The dog gave out a low whine and flattened itself to the ground, whimpering and growling.

"You're going to go in there?" Robard asked.

"Yes."

Robard shook his head and chuckled.

"Don't laugh. You're coming in with me." I had no intention of entering that place without someone to watch my back.

"Oh, don't worry. I wouldn't miss this for the world," he said.

"Maryam, would you kindly wait here and keep watch? Give a shout if anyone shows up. Besides, I don't think The Dancing Fig is any place for a . . . well . . . let's just say it's probably best that Robard and I go in alone."

Maryam smiled and agreed to wait. Moving a few steps away she took a position inside the doorway of a building, giving her a good view of the street in both directions. The dog followed along and curled up at her feet.

I handed my short sword to Robard. "You might find this more useful than a bow or your dagger at close quarters," I told him.

He held the sword out in front of him, as if I'd handed him a bouquet of flowers or a small kitten. "What are you going to use?"

"I still have the battle sword." I adjusted it so that it lay across my back at a better angle, making it easier to draw.

Robard saw the logic of my suggestion and buckled my sword around his waist.

"Shall we?" I asked.

Entering The Dancing Fig we discovered that the inside looked even worse than the outside. The smell hit us like a punch in the face, an ugly combination of spilled ale, burned meat and unwashed men. My eyes began to water, and I waved my hand back and forth over my face for a few moments until I grew used to the odor.

It was dim inside, with light from a few oil lamps placed here and there along the walls. Some candles were lighted, placed on the few tables that took up the main part of the room. Along the back wall was a wooden bar with an open doorway behind it. A dark-haired man stood behind the bar, surveying us as we entered.

Most every table was occupied. A few of them held a single man drinking alone. Some of them were surrounded by small groups holding loud conversations. No one, except the man behind the bar, paid us any attention.

"Now what?" Robard whispered.

I didn't answer, walking across the floor to the bar. Robard stepped to the side of the door, but kept his eyes on the occupants of the main room.

The man watched me approach, but his expression never changed. His eyes were hooded, and he appeared tired and uninterested in anything I might have to say. Unless I wanted to buy some ale, I expect he looked forward to the shortest possible conversation.

"Excuse me, sir. I'm seeking passage by ship out of Tyre, ideally to England. Do you know someone who might help me?"

The man stared at me, then at Robard still standing by the door, and said nothing.

"Excuse me. I'm looking for a ship." I spoke more loudly this time.

Still nothing.

A thought occurred to me. I reached in the satchel, feeling around for the bag of coins that Sir Thomas had given me. I found a small one and placed it on the bar in front of me.

The man's hand shot out for the coin like a cobra, but I grabbed his wrist while his fingers clutched the coin. The man glared at me, eyes narrowed, but I held his gaze.

"A ship?"

He nodded in the direction of a man sitting at a small table along the far wall. I let go of his wrist, and he quickly secreted the coin somewhere beneath the bar.

"Thank you," I said.

Picking my way through the tables and chairs I reached the man sitting at the table along the wall. He was old, with white hair, or what might once have been white hair had it not been covered in dirt and grime. He wore a simple shirt and woolen leggings, but it was impossible to tell their color, they were so torn and dirty. He smelled like he'd been in the ale for a while, and indeed a dark jug sat next to a small cup on the table in front of him.

He stared up at me when I reached his table, closing one of his eyes as he tried to focus on me.

"Who're you?" he asked.

"I'm told you have a ship. I'm interested in passage for me and my friend. I can pay. However, we need to leave right away. Tonight, if possible, first light at the latest. Can you help me?"

"A ship, you say? Aye, I've a ship. A fine ship she is. And I'm leaving tomorrow. Tomorrow without fail. You got money?" He squinted at me again.

"Yes, I have money for both of us. How much will it cost?"

He told me and I laughed. He wanted an outrageous sum. He tried again to focus on me with his other eye, but it appeared to not be working correctly, so he squinted at me again.

"Thank you. I think I'll ask elsewhere." I turned as if to walk away.

"Hold on there, laddie. I may be able to work with you on the price. If you're willing to pitch in and do some rowing when the wind is down. Help out with the rest of the crew loading cargo and whatnot, we can make it work," he said.

I stopped. I had never done anything like this negotiation before, but I knew that I shouldn't give in easily.

"If we do as you say, then how much?" I asked. He told me.

"That's an outrageous price. I'll look elsewhere, thanks," I said.

"Wait! All right. Fine! If you give me the money up front we can make a deal," he said.

"I'll give you half the money now, the rest when we reach our destination," I countered. "And I'll give you an extra five crosslets if we go to the ship now, immediately, and weigh anchor."

The man—his name was Denby, he told me—sat thinking for a minute. At least I thought he was thinking. He could have been sleeping for all the ale he had drunk. He pointed to a group of men sitting at a table in the corner. They looked every bit as grimy as he did.

"That's me crew," he said. "I'll have to get them to agree."

"Do it then," I said. "Tell them there are thirty regiments of Saracens about to attack Tyre at any moment. Then the city will be closed down. No one will get in or out."

Denby's head straightened up, with his one eye now focusing sharply on me. "Is that true?" he asked.

"Yes, it's true. I would urge you to leave tonight or risk being caught in a city under siege."

Denby sat back in his chair. It looked painful for him to have to concentrate this much. "Might as well," he said, picking up the jug on his table, first shaking it, then tipping it over the cup. Nothing came out of it. "I'm out of ale and money."

Standing up it took him a moment to be sure he had his balance and wasn't going to fall over. He stumbled over to the table, speaking to the men in low tones. There was some grumbling, and there were curses and a few hotly exchanged words, but after a few moments the three men finished their drinks, stood up and made their way to the door.

Denby staggered back to me. "If you and your friend are ready, we can go now. Our longboat is tied to the dock outside. I'll be taking the money now," he said.

"I'll give you the money when we are on your ship and under way, not before," I replied.

He squinted at me again. "I'm beginning to think you don't trust me."

"Let's go," I answered.

Denby shuffled across the floor, barely keeping upright until he reached the door. He passed through it with scarcely a glance at Robard, who looked at me with his eyes wide, as if wondering if I was crazy enough to book passage with a drunken boat captain. Given Denby's condition, I could only imagine what the ship must be like. But we needed to get out, and our options were few.

"Please tell me you know what you're doing," Robard whispered to me as we left The Dancing Fig.

"Of course. It's all under control. I just booked us passage on a ship to England. We leave tonight," I told him.

"I'm not going anywhere with that drunkard," he replied.

"Robard, I know it's not perfect. But we need to get out fast. Come with me. I can pay for both our voyages. If you stay here, Sir Hugh could capture you, or it will take you months to get home by land. With luck we can get back to England in a few weeks."

Robard stood still. Down the dock, Denby and his men had climbed into the longboat and were ready to depart. I waited, hoping he would agree. Hoping that I wouldn't have to beg him to come with me.

But the decision was made for him, for at that very moment, Maryam ran up to us. "The guards!" she said. "They're coming!"

30

hey're a ways down the street, moving slowly and searching the alleys. At least six men-at-arms. They'll be here in minutes." At her feet, the dog whined, circling about us as if it wished to move us in a direction, any direction, as long as it led to safety.

"Robard? What do you say? Are you coming with me?" I asked.

"Well, I don't have much choice now," he said with a measure of disgust, starting down the dock to where the longboat was tied.

"Aren't you going to say good-bye?" Maryam called after him.

He turned with a puzzled expression on his face.

"I already said good-bye once. Good luck to you, Assassin. I thank you for rescuing us from the jail," he said. "And for not killing us."

"Good-bye, Archer. Keep practicing with that bow. You can't count on a lucky shot every time," she said.

Robard's face went red, and he muttered something I couldn't hear and stomped off down the dock, climbing into the boat.

Maryam smiled as he retreated.

I followed after Robard, and Maryam walked quickly alongside me. The dog was still growling and whining as we approached the boat.

"Well, Maryam, unlike last time I guess this is really good-bye. Thank you for coming to our aid," I said. "Please take care of yourself. I hope, well, someday perhaps we will meet again."

"Good-bye to you, mysterious Tristan of the Templars. You should know that the Templars are greatly feared among my people. You do their Order proud. You are brave, but more important you are noble. I believe that Allah shines his light on you. Take care, my friend," she said.

By then we were next to the longboat, and unexpectedly Maryam reached out and took me in a tight embrace. Her arms were fast around my shoulders and my face was pressed into her hair, which still smelled of sandalwood. I felt dizzy and a little uncomfortable. I did not know how long we stood there, but it felt like an hour passed. Finally the crew and captain waiting in the boat, and Robard as well, began to cough uncomfortably. Maryam released me, touching my face with her hand. I felt my cheeks burning, standing there speechless, not knowing what to do next.

"Tristan," said Robard. "Tristan.

"Tristan!" he hissed.

Finally I came to my senses. "Yes?"

"The boat. We need to escape. Bad men are after us? You do remember?" He smirked.

"Uh. Yes. Of course," I replied, climbing into the boat and sitting next to Robard. The dog began whimpering and finally let out several low barks. She moved up to the edge of the dock, making as if she wanted to jump into the boat with me.

"No, girl. Stay," I told her. But she only whined more.

The captain pushed off with an oar. The crew began rowing, and we slowly moved parallel to the dock. Maryam and the dog walked with us for a ways.

There was a shout from the end of the dock. "Halt! Don't move another step," a voice hollered from the darkness. I recognized Sir Hugh's high-pitched voice immediately. The sound of running feet could be heard coming up the dock. Maryam was trapped.

"Go back," I yelled to the captain.

"No, sir," he said. "I want no trouble with those soldiers."

I glanced back at the dock. Maryam stood frozen, and the dog was jumping and barking as the men drew closer.

"Robard, hold them off," I said.

Robard stood and strung his bow in a single motion. In seconds he had pulled an arrow from his wallet, took aim and let it fly toward our attackers. It landed a few feet in front of Sir Hugh, who for once in his life was leading an attack. Admittedly an attack on a single girl and a small dog, but still he took the front.

When the arrow thunked into the dock, he skidded to a stop.

"Halt immediately! In the name of the Knights Templar I demand you return at once!" he shouted.

Robard answered with another arrow, which landed even closer. Sir Hugh took several steps backward and barked an order to his men. "Crossbows!" Now we were in trouble.

The men-at-arms sheathed their swords, pulling their crossbows from around their backs. They began to load the bolts. Our time was running out. The only advantage lay in the fact that crossbows are difficult to load. Once they release a bolt, it can take a minute or more to reload.

Maryam had drawn her daggers and stood crouching at the end of the dock, ready to go down fighting. The dog was yapping furiously. The crew had started to really pull at the oars, and we moved farther from the dock.

"Go back!" I shouted again at the captain.

"No, laddie," he said.

I pulled my sword and placed it at his neck. He gulped and his men stopped rowing.

"I'll give you two seconds to change your mind," I told him.

"Reverse! To the dock," he shouted to his crew.

He must have paid his men well, for they didn't hesitate, reversing the oars, and we moved slowly backward toward the dock.

"Robard! Watch the crossbows!" I attempted to keep one eye on Maryam and the other on the captain lest he change his mind.

The first bolt whistled at the boat, striking the side. But it glanced off, doing no damage.

Robard let loose with another arrow, and a second later I heard a scream from one of the men-at-arms and saw him crumple to the dock. We were still about ten feet away from Maryam.

"Maryam, we're coming!" I assured her.

She looked back at us and then at the men still several feet away down the dock. Without a word she backed up a little, took a running start and leapt through the air to the boat.

"Look out!" the captain hollered.

Maryam landed on top of Robard and me. Luckily Robard was not in the act of shooting or she might have been pierced by another of his arrows. We all landed in a heap at the bottom. The boat rocked back and forth, and for a moment I thought we might capsize, but then it steadied.

"Go," I yelled.

The captain and his crew rowed furiously. Sir Hugh and his men reached the end of the dock. Two of them dropped to their knees, taking aim with their crossbows. I pushed Maryam to the side and both of us crouched beneath the gunwales of the boat.

Robard, however, stood, drew another arrow from his wallet and let it fly at the dock. It landed in a post about six inches from Sir Hugh's head. Darn the luck. He shouted in surprise and very quickly moved behind the men-at-arms.

With each second we gained distance. Another bolt from a crossbow whistled toward us but missed again, landing in the water beyond the bow.

I noticed something moving in the water by the dock that caught my eye. The dog. It had jumped off the dock and was swimming toward us.

Maryam saw it too. "Tristan, look!" she said, pointing.

"I see it," I said. "Captain!"

"I'm not going back again, not against those crossbows. Strike me down if you must, but I'll not risk my life and crew for a mutt," he said.

The dog bobbed and floated in the water, struggling mightily to catch up to us.

We were almost out of range of the crossbows.

Without thinking, I stood up, unbuckled my sword, dropped the satchel to the floor and dove into the water. I was an adequate swimmer, having learned in the river near the abbey, but I hadn't swum in a long while.

I kicked forward, plowing through the water with my arms, trying to keep my head up and the dog in sight. It was difficult and I slipped beneath the water a few times to confuse the bowmen, but I slowly closed the gap.

When I reached her, the dog was nearly exhausted. I grabbed her in one arm and turned toward the boat. I was in range of the crossbows, and although I was completely disoriented in the water, I could hear Sir Hugh shouting, "Shoot him! Shoot him!" The bolts whistled over and around me in the water but miraculously none of them hit me.

I paddled away with my one arm, the dog clutched tightly in the other, kicking furiously. Off somewhere I could hear Robard shouting to the captain, but I was tired and the boat slipped farther away.

I drifted under the water once, then again. Each time I burst to the surface spitting out water. My legs were cramping and I had no strength left. Exhausted and not sure I was going to make it, I came to the surface only a few yards away from the boat. With every ounce of strength I had left, I kicked mightily. It was not enough.

I felt something hard knock me on the shoulder. Reaching up I grabbed a piece of wood and was pulled through the water. It was Robard leaning over the side of the boat and pulling me in with his bow.

Hands lifted me up and over the side. I slumped to the floor with Robard holding me up by the shoulders. He shouted at the captain to get moving, and Maryam took the dog from my grasp. She set it on the seat in front of us, and it shook the water from its coat, looking at me and barking happily, its tiny tail wagging. It jumped into my lap eagerly licking my face. I couldn't help but chuckle.

When I could lift my head, I looked back at the dock to see Sir Hugh pacing back and forth yelling at his men to "find a boat!" but they grew smaller and smaller as we moved farther out into the harbor.

Safe at last.

ON THE SEA

he crew took up a fast rhythm as the oars sliced through the water. We moved past the ships lying at anchor, around several galleys and barges, until we came to the last ship, anchored farthest from the shore. Well, at least the captain *called* it a ship. It looked as if it could barely float. Of course the lighting was poor. The moon had set, and only a small flame came from the torch the captain had lighted. As we drew closer, I saw that it was true. The ship was a wreck.

First of all, it was small. Very small. A quarter the size of a Templar ship, and with very little draft, so it sat high in the water. Three oars reached out from each side, and a single mast held a tattered sail hanging from it. The railing around the main deck was broken in places, and it looked all in all like it might sink at any moment.

"You booked us passage on this?" Robard said, his voice full of disbelief.

"Well. Yes. But looks can be deceiving," I replied. In fact, I thought in this case, looks were perhaps as accurate as could be. I had a horrible feeling about it.

As the longboat pulled alongside the ship, one of the crewmen scampered up the anchor line, and in a few minutes a rope net came over the side. We climbed aboard. Standing on the deck of the ship I saw that it was even worse than I had first thought. After the captain fired several torches to give us light to see by, I wished we had stayed in the dark.

The deck was warped and rotting. Several of the boards were curved up at the ends. The sail was in terrible shape. It looked to have more holes than fabric. And it stank—an odd combination of unpleasant odors.

While the crew hurried about in an effort to get us under way, the captain approached me. "You can stow your gear below if you wish," he said. Since the smell on deck had already made me nauseated, I didn't believe the hold would be any better.

"No, thanks," I replied. "I think we'll sleep up here on the deck."

"Suit yourself. I know she doesn't look like much, but trust me, she'll get you where you want to go. Eventually. Long as you're not in a hurry, she'll do you fine. Now, you owe me some money. Don't forget you're going to have to pay extra for the dog and the girl," he said. "An extra ten crosslets each should do."

"You'll get an extra five crosslets total and be happy with it," I answered.

The captain started to protest, but with a hiss from Robard, and seeing the venom on his face, he decided not to press the issue. I felt around inside the satchel until I found the bag of coins. Turning my back to the captain, I counted out half the promised price and handed it over. There was no sense in letting him know how much money I had. I vowed then and there that the satchel would never leave my side while we were aboard ship. The three crewmen lowered the long oars into the water, and slowly the ship began to move. The captain also took a position on one of the oars. With each stroke of the oars, the little ship crept closer to the mouth of the harbor. The eastern sky was starting to lighten, but the stars were still magnificent, and for a moment I was captured by the beauty of the night sky.

The thought of Sir Hugh managing to rouse a ship to give chase intruded on my reverie, and I began pacing the deck.

"Can't you go any faster?" I asked the captain.

"We're short some crew. If you and your friend there take an oar, that'll even things out and we'll go faster. We can't raise the sail until we clear the harbor," he said.

Robard, who was standing by the mast, snorted, pulling at the tattered sail.

"Yes. Raising this sail. That will certainly help," he said.

"Besides, if we raise sail now, we risk running her up on the rocks at the mouth of the harbor. Wouldn't want that. Best to row around them," the captain said.

Rocks? Why were there always things to vex me on a ship? I hated ships.

With a heavy sigh, I moved behind one of the crewmen and took an oar. Robard did the same and now the oars were fully manned.

"Grab hold of this oar here, missy," Denby said. "Someone's got to man the rudder now. It gets tricky around these rocks."

Maryam switched places with the captain without complaint. He took the rudder, and for the next several minutes we did nothing but rock back and forth to the rhythm of the oars. A short while later he gave the order to raise sail and two of the crewmen hoisted the canvas, securing the rope holding the sail to the railing. It was a small sail, simply hung from a crossbeam tied to the top of the mast, but it did catch what little breeze there was, and we began moving faster.

For the rest of the early morning we sailed and rowed toward the west. I kept a sharp watch for pursuers but saw none, and slowly began to think we had finally escaped Sir Hugh. If there truly were Saracen patrols spotted near the city, as we had heard in the jail, perhaps he would be unable to divert men and resources to come after us. But he would try to avoid the battle, coward that he was, and get out the fastest way possible without arousing suspicion or calling attention to his cowardice. He would most likely try to escape by ship or ride farther west before the city was encircled, under the guise of gathering reinforcements or alerting other Templar Commanderies of the coming attack on Tyre.

That would disguise his real purpose, however. He at least suspected that I had the Holy Grail or knew where it was. Sir Hugh would be coming for me. Maybe not right away, but he would not give up. I needed to make sure I got to Rosslyn before he did.

Morning dawned with no other ships in sight. We ate a morning meal of hard biscuits and some dried fish. The fish was nearly inedible to us but the dog seemed to enjoy it. The provisions on the ship were paltry and disgusting. There were several barrels of dried figs and dates aboard, so at the very least we could survive on those.

The next thing was to decide what to do with Maryam. Each gust of wind took us farther from her home. We discussed it among ourselves, and finally agreed to try to put as much distance between Sir Hugh and us as possible. Then, when the time was right, we would find a port city and secure Maryam passage on a ship back to her homeland.

We slept during the morning, finding a tiny shady spot in the shadow of the sail, and took turns dozing on the deck. I did not trust the captain or his crew. And Maryam, Robard and I came to the same silent conclusion that one of us would need to keep watch at all times.

That was how we passed the first three days aboard the ship. The captain wanted to put ashore at Cyprus to see if he could find more passengers or arrange for cargo to be transported, but an extra five crosslets persuaded him to keep sailing. I didn't want to stop so close to Tyre and give Sir Hugh time to catch up. Any time we spent not moving toward England was time he could narrow the chase. Anywhere we stopped, people would see us, leaving a trail for him to follow.

Toward dusk of the fourth day a storm rose. All day long the crew and captain acted strangely. The captain took the rudder, constantly looking off to the east, studying the sky as it filled with dark and ominous clouds. He changed course in the afternoon and we began sailing almost straight north. Since we were still in the Mediterranean, it was likely that we would hit land soon if we kept heading in that direction. The wind picked up considerably and the little ship plunged forward. What had been gentle swells became larger waves, and the ship heaved and crashed over them.

As we sailed along, the captain muttered to himself about "the ugly head" over and over. I thought he might be crazy, so I asked one of the crewmen what he was referring to. There was a tale, the crewman said, of an ancient god who cut off the head of his enemy, tossing it into the sea where it drifted for eternity. As it floated in the sea, the head would rise and fall with the waves. The legend said that if the head faced down, the waters would be calm, but when it showed its ugly face skyward, then a horrible storm would follow. The crew feared that somewhere on the sea, the ugly head now faced toward the sky.

Robard snorted when he heard this, cursing me for hiring a captain who was both drunk and insane.

"The only ugly head here is his," Robard said, pointing at the captain.

A few hours before dusk, the winds died down and the waves settled somewhat, but it was only the calm before the real storm. As dusk approached, the sky went almost completely black without warning. Lightning crackled overhead. Rain fell hard and sudden, and we were soaked through in minutes. The wind roared from the east, and the ship tossed in the waves that crashed over the bow of the boat.

Captain Denby and a crewman lowered the sail, giving each of us a length of rope.

"You'd better tie yourself to the railing. You don't want to get washed over," he shouted over the wind.

With no argument from us, we looped the rope over the railing and around our waists, tying it fast. The dog began whimpering. There was no way to secure her to anything, so I scooped her up in my arms, and she quieted as I held her.

The thunder and lightning came again and the rain fell harder. The captain yelled orders to the crew, but it seemed no one was listening, and indeed there was little they could do. The ship was at the mercy of the storm.

Up and down we went, splashing and crashing through the waves. It was a good thing we were lashed to the railing or we'd most certainly have been washed overboard. The dog began fidgeting in my arms, so I loosened my tunic, stuffing her down inside; she lay against my chest with just her face peering out.

I checked my ropes and held fast to the railing. The satchel was secure on my shoulder, but I felt it again to be sure. Robard was shrieking at the top of his lungs, curses and requests for the storm to do things to itself that were most likely impossible. Maryam said nothing, but I saw the worry on her face. She had had no choice but to come with us, since Sir Hugh would have had no qualms about killing her, I'm sure, and she was miles away from her home and her people, very likely to drown in the ocean.

There was a mighty thunderclap and the wind gusted hard against my back. Thunder boomed and lightning flashed. The air around us went bright white. In that instant a loud crack shook the ship, and I looked up to see that lightning had struck the crossbar. It had snapped, and now hung in place by only a few splinters. The wind whipped it back and forth until it finally gave way, crashing down toward us.

"Look out!" I shouted over the noise and wind.

Shoving Maryam as far to the left as her rope would allow, I pushed myself against Robard in the other direction. The crossbar splintered on the railing between Maryam and me. Pieces of it flew in every direction, and I howled as a large splinter pierced my calf. The dog wiggled, thrashing inside my tunic, and I clutched my chest with one arm, trying to calm it.

The railing was smashed and only Robard remained tied to it. Just then the ship pitched wildly in the waves and I saw the bow cut into a huge swell. The front of the ship rose until it was pointing almost straight up in the air. I heard shouts from the crew, but the wind was so strong and the rain so hard in my eyes that I couldn't see them anywhere.

I heard a screech from behind me and turned in time to see Maryam plunge into the water. Then the ship dipped again, righting itself. The wind punched me to my knees and I slid along the deck in the same direction. As I tried to stand, the ship suddenly pitched below me and the deck rose up again, slamming me onto it back-first. I felt with my arm for the dog, who was quivering and scared but still tucked safely inside my tunic.

"Tristan—Maryam! She went over!" Robard shouted.

"Help!" Maryam's voice was barely audible over the shriek of the wind.

I scrambled to my hands and knees, looking aft to find Maryam holding on to a piece of the anchor rope that was still secured to the deck.

"Hang on!" I yelled to her.

Staggering over to Robard, I handed him the dog. He took her in his arms, then tucked her safely inside his tunic. I tried to crawl back to Maryam, but the tossing of the ship made it nearly impossible. Inching closer, I saw that she couldn't hold on much longer.

Finally, with the wind howling around me and the rain pelting my face I made it to the rear of the ship. Maryam was just out of my grasp. I shouted at her to climb the rope hand over hand until I could reach her, but she was being dragged through the water, too terrified to loosen her grip on the rope for even a second.

I looked back at Robard, who was too far away to help, and I still couldn't see or hear the captain or the crew. Perhaps they were lost already.

"Maryam! You need to climb up the rope! Climb closer!" I shouted.

She just screamed and gripped the rope more tightly. The ship pitched upward again, and she disappeared beneath the water.

Then a strange thing happened. Over the noise of the wind and rain, I could hear a new but familiar sound. It was a faint humming that I had heard twice before, both times when I was in mortal danger. It was the sound of the Grail.

Time slowed. The bow of the ship came back down, and Maryam rose up out of the water. I grabbed for her but she was still too far away. I would never have believed what happened next had I not seen it with my own eyes. The Grail saved her.

The strap of the satchel flew off my shoulder, moving down my arm until I could grip it in my hand. As I held the strap firmly, the satchel, as if under its own power, slid outward until it was near enough for Maryam to clutch it to her. She released the rope, taking hold of the satchel with both hands while I pulled with all my might. The next thing I knew she was on the deck beside me, sputtering and spitting up water.

The strap to the satchel was twisted firmly around my wrist. I had no time to think about what I had just seen. The humming sound had stopped, but the storm had picked up intensity.

"Get back here! Hurry! You need to tie yourselves off!" Robard shouted from where he remained tied to the deck railing.

Maryam and I staggered to our feet but were knocked aside again as the ship dropped violently in the trough of a wave. We hit the deck, sliding along the slippery wet surface, and would have gone over again, but Robard reached out an arm to catch us as we slithered by.

He had enough of a length of rope left to bind Maryam about the waist. There was nothing for me to tie myself with. The wind howled and the water crashed over the ship as we bobbed up and down in the waves. Robard and Maryam were secure, and I held fast to the last broken piece of railing as we huddled together, praying for the storm to end. I feared the captain and crew had been lost. Or they were cowering in the hold, hoping to ride out the storm. Either way they were of no use to us.

For a few minutes, as the ship thrashed about, I thought we

might survive, until a particularly large wave washed over the side and I lost my grip. Tumbling across the deck I slammed into the mast. The ship teetered in the opposite direction, and I tried to grab on to the mast but missed, sliding across the deck away from Maryam and Robard.

"Tristan!" I heard them shout in unison. I didn't hear anything else, for the ship dove into another wave and I flew over the side, hitting the water with a jolt. It was cold, and I struggled to ride the waves and keep my head above water. The ship cantered away from me, but I heard another loud crack and watched the mast itself give way. There was a loud groaning sound as it tilted over, heading right for me. I kicked, lunging to get out of the way, but as it fell, the deck of the ship rose up and the mast hit it on the edge, snapping in two. The impact shattered the mast, and pieces of it went flying like arrows shot from a thousand bows.

The last thing I remember was a large piece of wood from the mast catapulting through the air, headed directly for me. I tried to dive below the water, but I felt it slam against my head and shoulders. After that I remember almost nothing. Nothing except a faint humming sound coming from somewhere I could not determine. I only knew it was familiar and comforting.

As the water closed over me, I remember thinking to myself that I had tried. Please forgive me, Sir Thomas. Please forgive me, but I did try.

Then the sea welcomed me into its dark embrace.

To be continued . . .

TURN THE PAGE FOR A PREVIEW OF

The
YOUNGEST
TEMPLAR

Book Two
Trail of Fate

THE SOUTHERN COAST OF FRANCE
OCTOBER 1191

I

A wall of ocean pushed me beneath the surface. I fought my way up into the air as the water rose and twisted violently, and tried to remember where I was. The tossing of the ship had swept me into the sea. I had no idea how long I'd been in the water but recalled seeing the broken mast come hurtling toward me. But I could remember nothing else. Over the sound of the wind I thought I heard Robard screaming, but it sounded faint and far away. Also, I tasted blood in my mouth.

The moon was completely obscured by the storm clouds. It was so dark that I couldn't see anything. As I came to my senses, I was completely disoriented by the sensation of the angry sea rising and falling. I could not tell up from down. I only knew I was wet. And frankly, a little tired of it all.

Bursting through the water's surface, I sucked in fresh air and felt for the satchel around my neck and shoulder, relieved to find it still there. The rushing sound of water behind me rose again, and I hollered out a curse. But the water was on me now, and I dipped violently in the trough before the wave threw me into the air. I hit the water on my back with a smack, and the breath was pushed from my lungs.

Another wave carried me up and then dashed me down again, and I collided with something hard. At first I thought it was a rock, but when the wave subsided, my feet touched the sea bottom. More waves crashed into me, but when they returned to the sea, I could stand. I didn't know which way to turn in the darkness with the howling wind and rain pelting my face. But then, as if God wanted to give me a fighting chance (or else keep me alive a bit longer to further torment me later), a flash of lightning flickered across the sky, and in a brief instant I saw land ahead of me: a shoreline, with trees and rocks in the distance.

Shouting in glee, I scrambled in the direction the lightning had shown me, the water growing shallower with each step, and before long it reached only my waist, then knees. With every last ounce of strength I splashed forward until the sand was under me, and I collapsed to the ground.

I woke to the taste of sand. It was salty and gritty, and light was coming from somewhere. Where were Robard and Maryam and the dog? Why couldn't I see them? But then I couldn't really see well at all, as my eyes were full of sand. I blinked to clear them and only partially succeeded.

It was relaxing to lie so peacefully, but I made the mistake of trying to lift my head, and the world spun away from me. I sank into unconsciousness.

When I came to again, I was no longer moving, but was still very wet.

Opening my right eye I wiggled my fingers, delighted to see that they worked. I'm not sure how much more time passed before I tried to move additional body parts. I clenched a fist. No pain.

Sore everywhere, I drove my fist into the sand, lifting myself up on one arm. It was daytime now, and the sun was high in the sky, so it must have been nearly noon. There was a line of trees about two hundred yards farther inland.

Pushing myself up to my hands and knees I winced when pain shot through my left knee. I had a vague recollection of hitting it on something the night before while thrashing about in the waves. My right elbow also throbbed, but didn't feel broken. When the dizziness passed, I finally stood.

My back wouldn't straighten all the way, and I wondered if my ribs were broken. I looked at the now calm sea. There was no indication of the fury it had unleashed on me the previous night.

Looking up and down the beach, I could see only a league or so in each direction before the shoreline bent out of sight.

"Robard! Maryam!" I shouted, but no one answered. Only the squawk of a few shorebirds disturbed the quiet.

"Captain Denby!"

"Little Dog!" Nothing. No answering bark.

With every intention of walking along the beach, I stumbled to the ground after a few steps, too tired to go any farther. Dropping on the sand, I quickly fell asleep.

When I woke, there were six people standing around me. Two of them were young women, four were men. Each held a horse by the reins.

All of them were pointing swords at me.

A Brief History of the Knights Templar

In 1104, a small group of knights under the command of Count Hugh de Payns of Champagne arrived in the Holy City of Jerusalem. Once there they offered their services to King Baldwin II, ruler of Jerusalem. Baldwin assigned them the task of safeguarding pilgrims who traveled the roads to and from Jerusalem. He offered them lodging in the Temple of Solomon. They became known as the Poor Fellow Soldiers of Christ and King Solomon's Temple, or simply, the Knights Templar. Templars could be identified by the bright red crosses that were embroidered on their tunics.

From these humble beginnings the Knights Templar became a major force in the world over the next two hundred years. Eventually, their order became enormously wealthy. Since they answered only to the Pope, they were outside the rule of monarchs. In their early history, they also conducted extensive excavations of the Temple of Solomon, and this has led historians and conspiracy theorists alike to speculate on what they may have uncovered there. Was it the Holy Grail? The Lost Ark of the Covenant? The One True Cross?

Ferocious in battle, the Templars usually aligned themselves with Christian forces of the monarchs who sent armies to the Holy Land during the Crusades. They were instrumental in many of Richard the Lionheart's victories during the Third Crusade, though by then Saladin had reoccupied Jerusalem and Richard was not able to reclaim it for the Christian world.

In the early part of the fourteenth century, King Philip of France, in allegiance with the Pope, declared the Templars to be heretics. In reality he wished to get his hands on their enormous wealth; but though he executed hundreds of Templars, he never found their vast stores of wealth and it remains missing to this day.

Author Interview

1. What inspired you to write this epic adventure novel?

I always try to write the kind of books I love to read myself. I really enjoy epic, sweeping yarns where the heroes are facing impossible odds, yet triumph by their friendship, their love for one another, and their inability to accept defeat.

I've loved the Crusades and this particular period of history since I was a small boy. Some of my favorite books were about Robin Hood and Richard the Lionheart and other heroes of the time. When I began writing, I just knew I had to set a novel or series there.

2. How much research did you do to make the book feel authentic?

A lot. A couple of years' worth at least. Really, since I've read so much about the Crusades over the years, you could say I've been researching this book my entire life. I've loved delving into the Knights Templar. They are a fascinating story in and of themselves.

The thing about research, especially in historical fiction, is that it can't come at the expense of the story. Most of the research that I did never ended up in the book. The characters are what matters in a novel, at least to me. If they don't work, then all the research in the world won't matter.

Discussion Questions

1. Read the prologue. Determine and discuss the main character and his quest. Predict why you think this duty has become a curse.

2. After reading chapter I, create a list of all the facts you know about Tristan.

3. Compare Tristan's life at St. Albans to his new life in Dover. Why do you think Sir Thomas chose Tristan? Would you have accepted the offer made by Sir Thomas?

4. Who are Tristan's enemies in the story? How are some who should be allies his enemies, and some enemies, his allies? Can you predict the difference as you read? What about in real life?

5. Do you think Sir Hugh despises Tristan for the initial incident with his horse or for something else? What evidence do you have? How is Sir Hugh's character revealed throughout the novel?

6. Describe what Tristan's role is in the battle in the Outremer. How does he act beyond his duties? Despite their success Tristan feels no glory. Why? How is he rewarded for his deed toward the king?

7. "The fighting usually starts when the talking ends. It lasts until the men grow weary of the fighting and seek to talk again" (p. 106). Is this still true with world conflicts today? Do you think it is "what men must do"? Is war ever necessary and justified?

8. Describe what happens in the city siege of Acre. Why does Sir Thomas send young Tristan off with his sword? What do you think happened to the knights who stayed? What is Tristan's duty and quest?

9. List the events that happened along the road to Tyre. Who are Tristan's constant companions on this leg of his journey? How is the Assassin not what they expect?

10. How is Tristan aided by the Grail along his journey? Does he begin to believe in the importance of the relic?

11. How is Tristan treated in Tyre? How does he escape? Why do you think he decided to bury the Grail rather than carry it into the headquarters of the Templar? How did this prove to be wise?

12. Explain how the Assassin ends up on the vessel to England. Do you think the Assassin will be safe in an English country? What do you think will become of the trio? Do you believe they will finish the quest together?

13. Which part of the novel was your favorite? What can you learn from Spradlin's story that you can use in the creation of your own stories? What makes a story great?

GLOSSARY OF TERMS

Al Hashshashin—A mysterious sect of Muslim warriors.

Beauseant—The battle cry of the Knights Templar. Loosely translated, it means "Be glorious!" Beauseant originally referred to the brown and white templar flag that was carried into battle.

Commandery—A building or compound where Templars live and train. Commanderies were located in almost every European country and throughout the Holy Land.

Marshal—The commanding knight of a regimento, the equivalent of a colonel in today's military.

Outremer—The Templar term for the Holy Land. It means "the land beyond the sea."

Regimento—A group of knights that were stationed at a commandery. They could number from 70 to 200 in residence.

Sargeanto—A knight who functioned as a leader of small squads of knights.